▲

A pair of 3.5-inch rockets detached from their pods, ignited and sped toward the enemy gunboat. Arizona Jim nosed up and pulled out of the pattern as Bobby Pruitt, leading Savoy Alpha, loosed his first two missiles. The river flashed past under the Merlin's gracefully contoured lift body and the jungle rose toward the nimble craft. At three thousand feet, Jim leveled out and began a wide turn, looking back to see the results of their first pass.

A monumental column of smoke, flame and water rose from the surface of the river, where the gunboat had been.

Twenty seconds later a bright, flashing missile detonated on one of their planes, blasting away all the overconfidence of the pilots. Jim stared disbelievingly. A 300 mph Soviet Hokum attack helicopter bore in on them firing...

▽

★★★THE★★★
LIBERTY
CORPS
#6 COSTA RICAN CHAOS

Also by Mark K. Roberts

THE LIBERTY CORPS

THE LIBERTY CORPS #2:
Maracaibo Massacre

THE LIBERTY CORPS #3:
Canal Zone Conquest

THE LIBERTY CORPS #4:
Korean Carnage

THE LIBERTY CORPS #5:
Poisoned Paradise

Published by
POPULAR LIBRARY

★★★ THE ★★★
LIBERTY CORPS

#6 COSTA RICAN CHAOS

MARK K. ROBERTS

POPULAR LIBRARY

An Imprint of Warner Books, Inc.

A Warner Communications Company

Special acknowledgments to G. M. Hoover for his invaluable assistance in creating this volume.

POPULAR LIBRARY EDITION

Popular Library® and the fanciful P design are registered trademarks of Warner Books, Inc.

The Liberty Corps is a creation of Siegel & Siegel Ltd.

Popular Library books are published by
Warner Books, Inc.
666 Fifth Avenue
New York, N.Y. 10103

 A Warner Communications Company

Printed in the United States of America

First Printing: December, 1988

10 9 8 7 6 5 4 3 2 1

This volume in the adventures of *The LIBERTY CORPS* is dedicated to the officers and men serving aboard the ships engaged in the unpleasant duty of patrolling the Persian Gulf. All *real* Americans are proud of your sacrifice.

MKR

HISTORICAL NOTE

In March, 1988, Nicaraguan troops of the Ejercito Poblanas Sandinista (EPS) entered the neighboring state of Honduras with the stated purpose of attacking Contra training camps. At the same time, reports in *Jane's Defense Weekly* and *National Review* disclosed that a major build-up of Sandinista troops had been observed along the border of Costa Rica. Sabre rattling? Or a rehearsal for an invasion?

CHAPTER
1

Marine Lance Corporal Owen Cooper adjusted his Sam Browne belt and stepped from the guard shack into a light drizzle, to render the hand salute to an officer entering the base. The 05 prefix on the parking permit number of the windshield decal indicated the occupant to be a Navy Commander. Even this bit of information failed to impress Lance Corporal Cooper.

At twenty years of age, Cooper faced the hardest decision of his young life. He had but a short while to contemplate it.

"That's a company Ah wouldn't care to tie up with when Ah get outta this chickenshit outfit," commented Pvt. Lemuel Baker, breaking into Owen's glum reflections.

"Humph!" grunted the corporal resentfully. "What's that?"

"Ain . . . Haven't you noticed those poor bastards?" Lem pointed with his chin to the near left corner of Defense Access Road and Yeomen's Hall Road, where the latter entered the Naval Weapons Center, outside Charleston, South Carolina.

In spite of the inclement weather, a City of Charleston Department of Public Service truck, in bright new day-glo orange colors, sat by the curb while a two-man crew labored over an old-fashioned streetlight standard. Inside the truck cab sat the foreman, his uniform perfectly dry as he spoke into a hand mike.

"Oh, yeah, Lem. I see what you mean." Owen's thoughts drifted away, back to the Tennessee farm, his father's ruined hip joint, and his kid brother, Oliver, facing all that work at seventeen...

"Yuh know, Ah ain..." Lem broke off and thought a new path through language patterns instilled from childhood by the Texas Panhandle. "Ah'm not real shore the City of Charleston has responsibility for those lights."

Owen snorted derisively. "You can bet those guys are sure. Especially in this weather."

Wishing his partner would shut up and leave him to his problems, Owen made his thoughts slide away again to his family. Those damn mules, why the hell did Pop insist on keeping them around? By God, if he had to leave his beloved Corps because of that treacherous bastard of a jack, he'd shoot him. Again he tried to reason through his best course of action, automatically stepping outside to salute another officer aboard the base.

"Those guys just don't act right, Coop, they's kinda furtive like," Lem returned to his theme.

Impatient, Owen shook water from the clear plastic cover of his service cap and waved a bulldog-jowled Gunny through. "Awh, give it a break, will ya, Lem? Those Public Service people won't be doing a damn thing they don't have to. They're Civil Service. It's the simple nature of the beast."

Owen felt a little guilty about snapping at the young Texan. Still, concern for his overworked mother, with the added burdens of a crippled husband and substantial medical bills, again took precedence. There was simply no choice. As the eldest son, it was his clear duty to apply for a hardship discharge. Somehow he'd make the farm pay for his father's new hip joint. Perhaps then the Marines would take him back.

"You can stop fretting, Lem," Owen observed. "They're leaving."

"Yup. About damn time. What could be wrong with a

simple streetlight that would take two men a full two hours to fix?"

Owen didn't make reply, again preoccupied with his family dilemma.

Because of a training schedule of seven days per week, the American Foreign Legion had regulations against civilian use of its ranges. As a consequence, when Col. Lew Cutler bought his wife, T.J., one of the new Heckler and Koch P7-M7 .45 autos the Legion had started to issue, he had to take her to the private ranges of the RPM Gunshop in Charleston. The occasion came about when Lew learned there was to be an addition to the Cutler family. T.J. had never fired anything larger than a .22 rifle and fell in love with the compact little autoloader when she found herself giving Lew a run on the twenty-five-yard pistol range.

"Well, you're only five points under me," Lew admitted grumpily when they wheeled in their targets.

"Give me another round and I'll tie you," T.J. offered eagerly.

"I don't know, honey, it looks to me like that drizzle's gonna work up into a full-scale downpour."

T.J. studied the sky. "Oh, I don't think so. At least not for another hour. C'mon, Lew, I'm just beginning to enjoy myself."

Lew sighed. "Alright. I'll have to buy some ammo, we used all the Legion issue."

Entering the store, Lew hailed the clerk who had sold him the weapon. "Looks like you're finally going to get into my britches for some cartridges."

"Nothin' I like better than doin' business wi' ya," came the reply.

Lew could barely make out the thick accent. An impish idea flashed and he spoke with a straight face. "Do you know what three things the Chinese and the South Carolinians have in common?"

"Naw, wha'?" the clerk bit.

"They worship their ancestors, eat a lot of rice, and speak a foreign language," Lew told him.

Fighting to suppress a smile, the clerk inquired, "Is that supposed to be funny? Whadda yu need?"

"A box of forty-five. Uh . . . those Federal one-eighty-five-grain JHPs ought to do. They're close to the Legion reloads."

"Say, why'nt yu leave yer brass fo' the cleanup crew, mos' ever'body does."

"I'm not *that* rich. Besides, I work for the Legion, regardless of my Regular Army status, and the Legion reloads a lot of its practice ammo. I'd get my hide blistered by the Headquarters Armorer Sergeant if I didn't bring these back."

"Soot yusel'."

Lew returned to a blissful T.J., who quickly reloaded and began to blaze away. At the completion of three more rounds, she had him by one more hole in the X ring. Lew looked like he could chew off the slide from his Hardballer. They continued to fire until only enough cartridges remained for T.J. to load her piece. T.J. couldn't resist twitting Lew about outshooting him, in the clerk's hearing, as they passed through the store to the curb.

Seated behind the gigantic rosewood desk in his huge, opulent office in the National Palace in Managua, Nicaragua, Daniel Ortega read through the ten-page report a second time. His close-set, beady black eyes sparkled as its full implication expanded in his mind.

"Yes," he said softly, gloatingly. "This will do nicely. Perhaps it will shut up the infernal yapping of those damned Russians. If we can't pay them in cash, the least we can do is gain them more territory." He glanced up and smiled broadly. With the sheaf of papers in his left hand he gestured to his Chief of Staff. "You've done a magnificent job, Arturo. I fully approve the entire concept. You didn't state . . . so I'll ask you now, how long before you can put this operation into action?"

General Arturo Ramon Jesus Maria Cardenas grinned like a little boy given a bag of candy. "Ten days, Excellency. Perhaps even less. The first elements are already on the move."

"Remarkable. Not only will we keep the Soviet bear mollified, we strike a blow that will garner us much favorable publicity worldwide and make the American *cabrones* out to be fools. See to it at once."

When they left the shop, Lew turned right from the driveway onto Belvedere Road, continuing to the traffic signal a half mile down the street. There he turned left onto Maine Road.

"Keep a close eye on how we're going, hon," he admonished T.J. "I want you to come out here and practice on your own. You can never tell when I might be gone and you'll need that H and K. Oh, damn!" Lew put the brakes to the Ferrari.

They waited out the signal at River Road, then continued straight on. Crossing the Inland Waterway Bridge, T.J. made an infrequent request. "Lew, take me sailing sometime soon. Before the, ah, baby makes sea swells more than I can handle."

"Sure, babe. Anything the little mother wants."

They jounced over the railroad tracks, then Lew speeded up until they reached Highway 17. Lew pointed the Ferrari Brute to the right and distant Charleston. The drizzle grew heavier, forming undulating sheets of dingy gray.

"Lew, it's such a cruddy day. Why don't we go out to Cat Cay and spend the afternoon and evening with Mark and Kathy Kelly. Second Cohort's got the weekend off."

"Good idea," Lew clipped. He snatched up the cellular car phone and rang up the Kelly number. Kathy answered.

"Hello, Lew. What's the occasion? Surely Mark hasn't got another interruption to his too-brief leave?"

"'Another'?" Lew inquired. "Here we called up to inform you of two guests for the rest of the day."

"Oh, that'll be great. But Mark does have an interruption. A special staff meeting Colonel Watie called. Surely you knew about that?"

"Oh? Ah, yes. Of course I did," Lew faked it. He hadn't the least idea of what that might be. "Uh . . . wh-what do you think of Mark's part in it?" he probed, hoping for enlightenment.

Always wary, Kathy avoided the verbal trap. "I don't, or at least, I can't. Mark hasn't given me any of the details. Except he did believe it had something to do with a very important issue."

It had to be Lew's day for being outdone by women. Half the Legion should be so security conscious. He gripped the cellular phone to the point of white knuckles. "Uh, yeah, sure. Look, we're almost back in the city. A run over to the Center and we'll take the eleven o'clock ferry. Be there in an hour and a half. Bye."

Lew gave the beast its head in a rumble of tuned exhaust. Damn superior women, he fumed silently. But, he had to admit, he loved 'em all.

In the sound- and bug-proof Staff Conference room at Legion headquarters on Corsair Cay, Colonel Norman Stand Watie faced his assembled officers. "Gentlemen, it gives me extreme pleasure to make this announcement. The first American Foreign Legion aircraft carrier will arrive a week from tomorrow. With the pressure brought to bear by our friend Ballard Armitage, and the staunch support of Admiral Josh Colton, the Navy managed to hurry a little, which advanced the delivery date. Coming along with her will be a *Spruance* class destroyer, an oiler, and three old frigates." He paused a moment to let the jubilation subside.

"Now for the bad news. The Navy is using a patchwork crew of oldtimers, who haven't served on these ships since they were youngsters in the Vietnam War. Worse, there is only one man in the tiny fleet that ever served on the ancient carriers. And *he* volunteered to come out of retirement to make the delivery. Fortunately, though he is now in his eighties, his service was as a flight operations officer. He can train our New Breed on how to plan training and combat missions, set up the Combat Information Center and the plotting room."

"Ah, Colonel," Lt. Col. Patrick Andrews asked. "Where

am I supposed to find the people to staff all these positions?"

"Like we did for the Fast Attack Flotilla, Andy. I want the staff to immediately withdraw all personnel with seagoing naval experience from the existing Tables of Organization and Equipment and form them into a naval unit."

Groans rose around the table. With the exception of McDade and Seagraves, none of the staffers were familiar with the Navy or the sea. Watie gave them a crooked, what-the-hell grin.

"That loses us two staff members," Chuck Taylor complained. "Also, the rank situation alone will be a bitch."

"Seagraves and McDade can't be taken from their normal duties," Watie answered him. "As to running the Legion Navy, they can damn well fake it. As to the ranks, hell, I was never able to make heads or tails of them. What's wrong with the way the Legion already does things? Why not a Corporal Machinist, or a Sergeant Sonarman? In other words, why confuse the troops when they'll have to be able to cooperate under combat conditions on very short notice?"

Arkady Gulyakin couldn't believe his good fortune. The old saying that if one wanted something done right, one should do it oneself, must have merit. His large, white teeth flashed in a thin-lipped smile of self-congratulation. His heartbeat accelerated as the light changed and the bright red sports car powered around the island and headed toward the main gate. Major Arkady Gulyakin of the *Komitet Gosudarstvennoi Bezopasnosti* brushed a lock of curly blond hair away from his forehead and concentrated on his task.

Timing to the exact instant, Gulyakin plunged his right index finger into the face of the glowing red button of the gray-black box he held. At the entrance to the Naval Weapons Center, a huge old, cast-iron light standard flashed white and faded to black smoke-shrouded orange. Sheared off, the top half jumped into the air and fell sideways, while heavy chunks of iron shredded passing motorists. Ears ringing, Arkady Gulyakin climbed into the front seat of the white Southern Bell van and adjusted his telephone company uniform. He gave the ignition a quick turn.

The engine fired at once and Gulyakin pulled away from the curb. All the way down the block he fought the impulse to turn back and use his cover to survey the kill.

CHAPTER
2

Humming a lighthearted ditty, Lt. Debbie Stovall-Hoover stepped into the G-3 coffee room with lunch, and a glimpse of the news, on her mind. As usual she was late arriving and the horrified, as usual, voice of Loretta Childs, local anchorwoman, was in full bay over the latest domestic disaster.

". . .—fifteen this morning, a terrific blast shattered the Yeomen's Hall gate at the Naval Weapons Center." The camera shifted to what was left of the guard shack, with the hood and grill of a mangled sports car sticking out of it. There it remained until an artful curl of smoke drifted upward. Then the scene panned left and found the rear half of the same car, wedged into the side of an old Buick with blood running steadily from a sprung door.

"Oh! . . . My . . . God!" Debbie's coffee cup shattered on the tiled floor and convinced the rest of the diners that what they saw was real. In the wake of the confusion she created, Debbie ran back to her office and dialed a number. "Pops, let me speak to Colonel Watie, quick. What? I don't care, don't you understand? Lew Cutler is dead. It's on TV right now."

". . .—lice say there is no indication it was an act of organized terrorism." Loretta Childs's mobile features

squirmed from her number six, "you-can-trust-me" expression to a full ten in the "oh-do-I-have-compassion" cate-
gory. Her tone of voice became downright sepulchral.

"At least eight persons died in this terrible accident. The
names of the victims are being withheld until notification
of the next of kin." She gave a heavy sigh and came up
with an impish smile.

"Now, on the lighter side, this year's winner of the
WCTV Dalton Hunter look-alike con—..."

Col. Watie snapped off the set and turned to face the
room. "Mark, you and Andy in particular...Hell, all of
you, were friends..." He swallowed hard. "There's no
doubt that was T.J.'s Ferrari. Thanks to those ghoulish bastards on the tube anyone could clearly see the Cat Cay
vehicle sticker on what was left of the windshield. So,
I...I...Goddamnit! Get the hell out of here and break
the news gently. Move it!"

Colonel Norman Stand Watie had to turn his back as his
friends and fellow Legion officers filed silently from the
room.

"You can take that 'Weather Underground' crap and
stow it," Lt. Col. Sam Seagraves managed to growl in a
whisper.

Standing with the rest of the staff and dignitaries from
the Pentagon and Regular Army establishment on the reviewing stand, Sam had seen his anger grow over the past
four days. Now, the solemn tap of muted drums, their barrels draped in black, seemed to place an irrevocable finality
to what had been the lives of two fine people.

Autopsy reports had revealed nothing remarkable. The
corpses of the two Marines, five civilians, including T.J.
Cutler and Col. Lew Cutler, did reveal a residue of certain
chemical compounds common t military high explosives.
But some of these, the police and other agencies were
quick to explain, could also be found in certain automotive
paint formulas. The FBI was looking into several of the old
anti-war groups of the sixties, on the assumption the blast
had been a random anti-military demonstration. Sam didn't
buy it, and neither did anyone else in the Legion. Yet,

before they did anything about it, they had to turn out to show their respects.

The funeral for Lew Cutler and his bride of less than a year turned out to be the largest occasion to date on Corsair Cay. To the surprise of everyone who knew the inside story, Lt. General Eugene Willowby and his wife attended also. The entire Legion paraded. From a distant peak, the highest on the island, a solitary piper skirled a mournful rendition of "Amazing Grace." Then, because it was discovered that Lew had been of the Clan MacDonald, he played "The Rape of Glencoe."

A century of Merlin 400s, totaling 150 aircraft, made a flyby, then hovered over the funeral procession as it progressed from the parade ground to the Legion cemetery. Here, only the closest to the deceased were admitted. The final salute was fired and three trumpets played "Taps" mournfully. There was not a dry eye, someone noted. Afterward, talk turned to finding out *who*. The why seemed obvious.

Arkady Gulyakin absolutely glowed. He had filed his encrypted report with Moscow Center immediately after the explosion, confident, as had been the Legion commander, that he had struck a telling blow to the Legion. Then he waited with trepidation for five long, silent days. This morning, along with the weekly communiqué, came two special, and quite remarkable, documents. The first was unguarded praise for his destruction of a major Legion asset, demoralization of the rank and file, and disruption of smooth liaison between the piratical American Foreign Legion and the Pentagon. The second was his long delayed, and highly coveted, promotion to *Podpolkovnik* (Lt. Colonel) in the KGB. Truly it marked an occasion to celebrate.

"Fyeodor Ivanovich," Arkady jovially called out to his second in command. "Bring a bottle of the Dom Perignon and two glasses. You and I must toast our success. Ah, also bring along a five-hundred-gram tin of the Baluga caviar."

Fyeodor Dobredyn raised shaggy eyebrows. Unlike his handsome superior, Fyeodor looked the part of a Hollywood stereotype KGB bully. His massive body rolled when he walked, not from fat, but solid brawn. Small, black, pig eyes glittered from a broad, flat peasant face. From a special pantry in their living quarters of the safe house in Savannah, Georgia, he obtained the caviar. The wine cellar provided the champagne. As an afterthought, he added a crystal bowl with chopped onion, another with hardboiled egg, and a plate with small, dry toast points.

"Congratulations, Comrade *Podpolkovnik*," he rumbled as he entered Gulyakin's study. A slight tic developed at the corner of his left eye when he brought in the silk lounging jacket and Cardin pajamas his superior wore. Such luxury, Dobredyn believed, was anti-Party.

"Thank you, Fyeodor Ivanovich. Now we have to lay plans for that Indian. *Borg*, ah, damn him, he never leaves that island, except when surrounded by the whole Legion, on the way to fight somewhere. Or to fly to Washington to a conference. Ah! That's the answer. We have a lot of friends in Washington. It should be easy."

Preceded by two frigates and the DD, the *Lexington* class aircraft carrier *Saipan* entered Corsair Cove. Because of her size and draft, she had to drop anchor two hundred yards inside the circular cove, rather than tie up at the dock. A detachment of the Legion band and the staff, with banners flying, met the first contingent of the Legion Navy. A blue pennant topped the commissioning halyard of the carrier, bearing the single white star of a Rear Admiral. *What the hell*? Stand Watie wondered. He'd heard nothing of this. A huge door on the third or storage deck swung wide and a group of blue-dungareed sailors swung out and lowered a spanking bright powerboat.

"By God, that's an admiral's barge," Lt. Col. Sam Seagraves blurted. "How'n hell did we get an admiral, along with our Navy?"

"We'll find out soon enough, I suppose," Col. Watie answered him. "What's the protocol for welcoming an admiral?"

"Uh ... I think it's ... six bells, six side boys, and two ruffles and flourishes," Sam answered.

"Bells?" Watie asked, incredulous.

"Bells," Sam affirmed.

"Where do we get bells?" Lt. Col. Andrews asked, a pained expression on his face. An RA man all the way, Airborne and Special Forces at that, he had a decided prejudice against things nautical.

"A triangle will have to do this time," the M/Sgt. Band Master informed the staff a few moments later.

"Maybe they brought their own," Maj. Mick Orenda offered hopefully.

The small, spit-and-polish, bright-brass boat reached the dock. Two spiffily dressed crewmen held on to securing lines, while the coxswain kept the craft motionless by deft handling of throttle and tiller. A short, incredibly thin, hatchet-faced individual, in the uniform of an admiral, climbed the gangway with the ease of a monkey. The triangle sounded and he scowled. His aide reached the pier and stood beside him, paper in hand.

"Rear Admiral Thomas O'Fallon," he read aloud. While the band played the two ruffles and flourishes, he marched briskly to Col. Watie, saluted smartly, and handed him the paper.

"Attention to orders," Watie read off in his turn. "'Be it known that effective One June in the year two thousand, Rear Admiral Thomas O'Fallon, USN Retired, assumes temporary command of the American Foreign Legion Naval Service, for the purpose of training duty implementation, and shall have all the rights and privileges afforded his rank and station. By authority of the Commander in Chief. Signed, Walter O. Stennis, Secretary of the Navy.' Welcome to Corsair Cay, Admiral."

"Urrrumph! You need a regulation bell installed here. At least you got the side boys and ruffles and flourishes right," came the first, grumpy words from the new Legion officer. "Now that I'm in command here, things will be made shipshape soon enough."

"Ah, begging the Admiral's pardon, sir," Stan Watie began. "Let me introduce myself. I'm Colonel Norman Stand Watie, Commandant of the Legion."

"Aarrgh! Ground-pounders. Isn't a one of you ranks

above able-bodied seaman with me. But you'll be doing things the Navy way right smartly."

"Excuse me, Admiral," Watie interrupted again, his temper rapidly rising toward the live steam point. "As Commandant of the Legion, it is *I* who command here."

"We'll see to that later," Thomas O'Fallon said offhandedly. "For now, get yourself and these people into proper dungarees and turn to with the work party for loading these ships."

Those familiar with Norman Watie recognized the danger signals; large head canted slightly to the right, pugnacious jaw out-thrust, eyes ablaze, with a pink tinge that would turn the whites scarlet in full rage. They waited, uncertain in this situation. Col. Watie spoke slowly, in a low and moderate tone.

"May I speak with you over here for a moment, Admiral?"

"Eh? Won't this do well enough? I believe I just issued an order?"

"Yes, sir. That's what I wanted to bring to your attention."

Adroitly, Watie steered the naval officer out of hearing of the staff. Unaccustomed to being crossed at anything, O'Fallon bristled. Stiff index finger extended from a balled fist, he started to read the riot act to this insolent ordinary seaman. Watie silenced him momentarily with a harsh tone.

"Admiral O'Fallon, unless I am terribly mistaken, I just read an order placing you in command of the Legion Carrier Task Force. As such, while on board any of your vessels, your orders are supreme. But you, sir, are on Corsair Cay, where *I* command. As Legion Commandant, I am in command of *all* Legion elements. That includes the Task Force."

"I'm afraid you've greatly misinterpreted those orders. General Willowby and Collingwood concurred with Admiral Creighton, the CJCS, and the Secretary of the Navy that I was to come down here and take charge. Naturally, the first order of business is to have a general shakedown, clean house, and appoint a new officer corps of my choosing. Men who will, ah, work within the system." The malice in his icy words left no doubt as to his intentions, or their source.

"*Wrong!*" Watie snapped, fuse sputtering close to the detonator. "That order was written by the President of the United States, our Commander in Chief. Not by the Secretary, nor the Chairman of the Joint Chiefs of Staff, nor Generals in the Pentagon. It means *exactly* what it says, and not a word, hint, or innuendo more. Outside of those assigned to Task Force duty, not one of my men will wear Navy blue dungarees, or play stevedore for you, let alone my Cohort officers or staff members. Also you will not, I say again *will not*, issue any orders to Legion personnel on this or any other land facility or beachhead, except for those in the Task Force. With the exception of a direct order from the President, your orders will come from me."

"That will be rectified soon enough. In the meanwhile, I strongly recommend that you follow my orders."

Watie clapped the palm of one hand to his cheek, aware of the persistent urge to have done the same, only harder, to Admiral O'Fallon. "It appears you haven't heard a word I said. In my office is a telephone with a direct link to the White House. If you'd like to join me, we'll use it now. If not, I suggest you return to your flagship and make your needs regarding supplies known through channels to my G-Four."

Tight-faced, lips white with fury, Admiral O'Fallon choked out splinters of words. "I think a talk with the President will resolve this quickly enough."

When they came out of the Headquarters, Col. Norman Stand Watie exhibited a jovial, expansive mood. "Well, then, I'll arrange a spacious house for you on Cat Cay. We'll have to bring down Mrs. O'Fallon right away. And, ah, Admiral, please join me for dinner this evening. Nothing formal, but we *will* have your goddamned bells working."

CHAPTER
3

Gulls made their usual impertinent noises and left their accustomed black-and-white deposits on every exposed surface of Corsair Cay. These included the motor pool, artillery and tank parks, and the firing range equipment. Although as ready to grouse as any soldiers, anywhere, any time, Legionnaires generally went willingly to their tasks. Yet, since the arrival of the Legion Navy, grumbling had increased. It had the sound of men who had lost their spirit, rather than of discontent. Efficiency dropped dramatically. What the Legion needed, Col. Watie knew, was something to help them get over their collective grief at the murder of their RA liaison, Col. Lew Cutler. The task force had it worse.

Inept and impressed men hardly exhibited a fulsome will toward their new labors. Although reprovisioned and made ready for a shakedown cruise, the ships remained in port or close to Corsair Cay. Relations between the Admiral and Col. Watie remained chill, if not icy, and the former soldiers of the Legion stored injustices, real and imagined, that fueled their resentment at becoming sailors. Fury began to creep into Col. Watie's evaluation of the situation. He decided to address the men in an attempt to clear the self-induced miasma that blanketed everyone.

"Soldiers . . . and, ah, sailors of the Legion. . . . " Oh, hell, he'd gotten off on the wrong foot already, Watie silently cursed. "We have suffered a great loss. Yet, in the midst of it, we've gained something we've greatly desired for a long while. We have our own naval arm, one with the equipment, weapons, and know-how to protect itself and provide support to our future operations. Fully one-fifth of our complement have naval experience. When you add those with prior service in the Marines of this or other nations, it reaches some thirty-one percent. It has always been the Legion's policy to utilize a man or woman in the best possible place. Now we can." Shit! He was losing them. Next thing they'd be yawning. "It won't be easy. But while we're at it, we'll also be doing something about the cowardly terrorist-style murder of Colonel Lew Cutler and our beloved T. J."

That brought down the house. Cheers and shouts, whistles and stomping feet shook the walls. Delighted that he had hit upon the right thing to say, Col. Watie decided to shut up while he was ahead.

A heavy explosion shattered the jungle night, startling even the most amorous bullfrog into silence. In the quiet that lingered, Dr. Herman Silberman jerked straight up in bed, eyes seeking the green glow of his digital clock through the ghostly haze of mosquito netting. A sudden spatter of small arms fire sent a chill along his spine. *Gewalt*! Surely this couldn't be what he had been told about. Certainly not what he had expected.

Herman Silberman, physician, surgeon, and idealist, had come to Nicaragua to help build a lasting peace. To help frame a better world. In their wisdom, the United States Congress had cut off all aid to the fascist Contras and they had withered on the vine. As a result, Daniel Ortega and the Sandinistas had managed to survive the threats of the nineteen-eighties. They needed all the dedicated men and women they could attract to their cause so they could extend their Marxist-Leninist principles of peace and order throughout Central America. Dr. Silberman had been an early and eager volunteer.

They had placed him in the back country, lowland jungle really, which he didn't mind. A month ago they had put him in charge of the medical needs at this remote station. Then, only days before, they had brought in the Compulsory Work Battalion. Another rattle of gunfire, closer now, propelled Dr. Silberman from his bed. He pulled on trousers, sandals, and a no-longer-white medical smock. The question kept pounding at him.

Who was this International Brigade that was supposed to temporarily occupy the area? More gunfire. With the thatch cover raised from a front window, Silberman could see the orange flickers of muzzle blasts. They moved toward the laborers' compound. These *can't* be the men he'd been told to expect. Automatic rifles opened up again. In the bright moonlight, Dr. Silberman saw a small, spherical object hurtle through the air and in through a window. A bright yellow flash followed and the explosion hurt the healer's ears. Then the screams began.

Dr. Silberman looked on in horror while the dark shapes of the attackers darted from hut to hut, lobbed in grenades, then fired their rifles to silence the survivors. Several figures detached themselves and headed toward the hospital and his quarters. As they came nearer, Dr. Silberman thought he recognized Sgt. Mendez and Lt. Guiron. But that couldn't be. They were part of . . . Utter dread ended Silberman's contemplation. Terror, and a strong sense of survival, drove him to the rear wall of his hut and he dived out the window ahead of the grenade meant to shatter his body and claim his life.

Adrenaline jolted his system and brought him to his feet. He started to run through the jungle, toward the envisioned safety of the San Jaun River. All that had happened seemed only too familiar. While his legs churned, Dr. Silberman marveled at how calmly he had received the word about the International Brigade. He accepted now that a part of his brain must have recognized what was going to happen. Yet in his zeal to see the advent of the brave new socialist world he had deliberately blinded himself to the obvious. As he ran, the screams of the tortured and dying haunted him. He hit the slippery mud of the riverbank before he expected it.

Propelled onward, although his feet had stopped moving, the good doctor found himself waist deep in the tepid water. To his left he heard a gurgling swirl and a soft splash. Could someone else have escaped? P-A-I-N, sharp, bright, and paralyzing, burst in Dr. Silberman's pelvic region.

Gagging, he fought against a forceful tug, and managed a short, shrill scream when a large, curved tooth pierced his scrotum and demolished a testicle. Another tooth finished the job the circumcision shears had begun in his infancy. A glowing image fought the numbness that mercifully filled his brain. *Crocodile!* It had to be. Dr. Silberman's knowledge of zoology acted to feed his growing terror.

A crocodile's jaws were so arranged that he could neither bite off nor chew. Simply put, they were tongs, serving only to seize. Its gullet opening was somewhat small, and since it could not chew, it must reduce its prey to gulp-size portions. So it did by rotting its food. In the last horrible moments of his dedicated Marxist life, Dr. Herman Silberman visualized his fate.

Drawn beneath the muddy brown water to slowly drown, he would be wedged in among some roots and left until decomposition had advanced far enough for the prehistoric monster who had seized him to slurp off suitable portions. Fully conscious, the humanitarian physician realized there would be no escape. The crocodile would not let go. Nothing could save him. The absolute finality of the crocodile attack wasted his last reserves. Dr. Herman Silberman had only time to let out a final wailing shriek before his captor dragged his head under the scummy surface.

Behind him, the last of the human butchery came to an end. Silence returned to the jungle night.

Major Honey Simmons stomped along the highly polished hallway of the Legion hospital staff quarters on Corsair Cay. If her mood hadn't made her mouth so dry, she would gladly spit. What the hell did that big, dumb Indian think he was doing? She raged in frustrated silence. First he makes arrangements for that stuffed-shirt admiral and his family, then ... then ... The very idea of turning that lovely house over to Grace Gantry. Didn't he know that *she*, not Grace Gantry, had dreamed of occupying it since before the architect made the drawings? Couldn't he see that she was ideally suited to be the First Lady of the Legion? Didn't the big, dumb brute know that he loved her?

And now he had the absolute, unmitigated gall to ask her to the housewarming. Well, by God, he couldn't treat her that way. She'd show him a thing or three ...

"Oh, hello, darling!" Honey warbled as she opened the front door. "I'll be ready in a shake. Come on in. I'm so excited at meeting Mrs. Gantry."

Damn the man, he always does that to me.

Arizona Jim Levin had finally succumbed to the magic of the Merlins. He'd learned to fly them back when the Legion had only two of the old 200 models, and had been sorely tempted. Yet, flying airplanes, even Merlins, hadn't fitted his self-image too well. Now, with a few more combat operations down the pike, the situation looked different.

Actually, it had been Colonel Watie's appeal for experienced combat infantry people with some flying time, that made the difference. The Merlin 400's principal mission was to be close air support for the grunts, and Jim agreed with his commander that grunts should fly them. His promotion to captain was another incentive, of course. All in all, it left him quite pleased if somewhat late.

Captain Levin burst into the conference room to discover he was to be the junior officer present. Already a light bird stood at the platform, Don Beisel, if Jim recalled correctly, pointing out the armaments on a huge enlargement photo of a Merlin 400. He concluded as Arizona Jim found a seat. When the other enthusiasts had seated themselves, the bulk of the CO entered and the men clattered to attention.

"Be seated. Gentlemen, we are gathered here to begin a massive reorganization of the Legion Support Centuries.

Item one is Legion Hotel and India. These armored car units will no longer be known as cavalry..." Col. Watie raised a restraining hand as Lt. Col. Gordon Rounding bounced to his feet. "If you please, Colonel Rounding, hear me out. Traditionally, cavalry has been the eyes and ears of the commander. In addition, they harass the enemy in his rear and exploit breakthroughs. We now have an arm that fulfills some of these missions better than light armor.

"Gentlemen, I am referring to the new Merlin 400s, which will become our cavalry."

By this time, Maj. Bob Fuller and Capt. Luis Enchausti were also on their feet, as red-faced as Rounding. Watie continued his lecture as Maj. Orenda grinned from the sideline.

"Henceforward, Charley, Hotel, and the India will be reinforced by our new Legion Lima, which will be organized around fifty of the new APCs, and twenty-four South African G-6 One-five-fives. They will form the heart of a Dragoon Regiment, or for the purist, an *Aulius*, the designation given to the Roman legions' cavalry. Why dragoons? Because they traditionally ride to battle and fight dismounted. Legion Kilo will be equipped with one hundred of these babies," he went on, tapping the giant enlargement with his pointer. "Major Orenda?"

As Maj. Mick Orenda took center stage, the commanders of Legion armor eased back into their seats. Dragoons? It did have a certain ring, but whoever heard of flying cavalry? On an easel to his right, Orenda displayed several large, glossy photographs of what appeared to be a wheeled version of the M-113 APC. Watie continued.

"One in five of these will mount that One-Twenty mike-mike mortar gun in the top forward ball socket. It is capable of either direct or indirect fire. This unit has a four-man crew, and carries a whale of a lot of ammo. The rest are equipped with a thirty mike-mike chain gun turret and the gun is stabilized, as is the One-Twenty mm on the first model. It carries a full squad of twelve men, in addition to its two-man crew. Every trooper in Lima will crew on one or the other of these models, APC or SP Gun, including the commander. The only exception will be the head-

quarters platoon." Watie waved a ham-like hand toward
Orenda. "As usual, the Major here came up with the basic
design, as well as the TO slots. Cadillac-Gage developed
and built the APCs. Now, to Legion Kilo, this will be five
platoons of Merlin 400s. Each bird will have a pilot, and a
crew chief who will also drive the maintenance and transport truck. Major repairs will be carried out by Legion
Delta. The crews will be supported by their own headquarters platoon in garrison, or by the nearest mess if dispersed in the field. Eventually, I plan to replace our Bofors
guns at Cohort level with these South African beauties, as
they are accurate out to forty klicks without rocket assist."

This pronouncement proved too much for Lt. Col. Otto
Von Shallenberg. He rose in protest. "For two years you
have preached the gospel, if you will, of no self-propelled
guns. Now suddenly you reverse your, ah, theology.
Why?"

Watie gave the English-born and -raised Kraut a friendly
smile. "That's true. I've been the prophet of doom regarding SP artillery. Let me point out that my objections came
from when there were only tracked vehicles for gun plat-
forms. As such, SPs were not cost-effective, not in acquisition, employment, or maintenance costs. Many of you
will recall the vast distances over which we had to maneu-
ver in the African campaign, and how many tracks were
lost to fatigue. Frankly, gentlemen, much the same applies
to armored personnel carriers. Our new ones, however, get
around that expense factor. Now, to the next detail. Employment of the Merlin 400s, and the training schedule for
the squadron's enlisted pilots and their ground crewmen."

That's what he'd come for. Avidly, like a lover takes to
his lady, Arizona Jim leaned forward, broke out pen and
note pad and listened intently.

CHAPTER
4

More powerful than the all-pervading odor of a jungle, the stench of bloated, rotting bodies hung in the hospital compound. The whirling blades of the helicopter rotors had not even wound down before the eager film crews spilled out onto the blood-soaked ground. Several of the more experienced cameramen and audio people gagged and tied wet handkerchiefs over their noses and mouths as swarms of buzzing, noxious insects settled back to their feasting. Most of the handsome, mobile-faced reporters sought places to bend over and vomit up the ample breakfasts and champagne they had consumed at the Sandinista military outpost before departing for this remote back country hospital.

"Set up over there first, Ed," one managed as he finished rinsing his mouth and spat out the sour fluid.

"Get a pan shot on those stacked corpses, Tim," another instructed. "I'll be right here by this body in the well. Zoom in on me and we'll take sound then."

"Right, Brian. I'll cue you," Tim responded tightly, more than a little green around the mouth. "Rolling now . . . speed . . . panning to the left . . . and coming up on you . . . audio rolling . . . and take it."

"This is Brian Bartlett, CBS News, from the ravaged

compound of the San Carlos mission hospital in Rio San Juan Province, Nicaragua. The terrible scenes you are witnessing are the result of a savage raid by mutinous elements of the International Brigade. What we have encountered here is nearly beyond description."

Bartlett's voice broke and tears began to stream down his cheeks. He prided himself on his ability to emote, particularly to cry on cue. He had wanted to be an actor and wound up working for Black Rock instead. Still, it served him well.

"This hospital was staffed by American volunteers, men and women who came to Nicaragua as living proof that not all Americans saw evil where none existed. Three nights ago, foreign mercenaries invaded this peaceful settlement and slaughtered the patients and medical staff. The barbarity of the scene is heartbreaking. Word of this atrocity did not reach the nearest army outpost until late last night. Immediately the Sandinista government launched a relief force. We arrived with them only minutes ago. Scenes of horror greeted us, sights of such awful nature that perhaps only survivors of the Holocaust could visualize the devastation. There has not been time to identify the dead, but the Nicaraguan commander informed us that he believed everyone had been murdered in their sleep."

In the background white-clothed Red Cross workers laid out corpses on black plastic body bags and cleaned faces in an attempt to make identifications. "One can but wonder at the motivations and treachery of these soldiers for hire who so callously claimed so many innocent lives . . ."

"Trent Jarmon, ABC News," another grim-faced reporter spoke into the mike in his left hand. "I have with me the Sandinista commander on the scene, Lieutenant Miguel d'Escoto. Lieutenant d'Escoto, can you elaborate on the information you had given us earlier?"

"Presidente Ortega de este atrocidad hagar de informa. El tiene mucho . . ." The voice of the interpreter at Trent Jarmon's side came in. "President Ortega has been informed of this atrocity. He has great sorrow for the murdered innocents. Particularly for the brave American medical personnel who defied their ruler's will to join in

the confraternity of social justice here in Nicaragua. Their
martyrdom will be avenged. Reports from our advance
scouts indicate that the International Brigade has crossed
over into Costa Rica."

"Wasn't the International Brigade loyal to the Sandinista
government?" Jarmon asked, straight-faced.

"Elements of it still are. It is believed that the mutinous
units were seduced into this course of action by CIA plants
within the ranks."

"I would suppose so," Jarmon said in as casual-seeming
an aside as he could contrive. "Are your troops going after
the perpetrators?"

"Nicaragua is a peace-loving nation. We would never
violate the borders of our neighbors, unless specifically
asked for assistance. You may be certain, though,"
d'Escoto continued through the interpreter, "that everything possible will be done to bring the miscreants to justice."

An excited noncom rushed up and spoke agitatedly,
oblivious to the camera and microphone. "*Teniente, el doctor Silberman no esta aquí.*"

D'Escoto paled slightly and licked his lips. "*Condena-
ción!* Search the jungle for him, Sergeant Mendez," he
continued in Spanish. "He must be found . . . dead."

Major Jay Solice had developed a headache going over
the latest intelligence reports from Central America. Fortunately for the Legion, there were many eyes willing to take
notice of events for a few Yanqui dollars. Unfortunately,
Jay contended, they all thought themselves great writers.
The material was tedious, and only rarely did he come
across a gem like the one he perused now.

"'There has been a recent, massive movement of prisoners,'" he quoted aloud, "'from Minos de Pis Pis, in Ze-
laya Province, Nicaragua, to the vicinity of San Carlos in
Rio San Juan Province.' Moe, get me an update on everything that's happened along the Honduran-Nicaraguan
border in the past three months."

Maureen Ellis, a Legion intelligence sergeant, quickly

located the desired data and brought them to Jay's desk. "Want some help, Major?" she invited.

"I could use it," Jay replied gratefully.

Together they went over the reports. After double-checking each other, the result remained the same. They found nothing unusual. Routine anti-communist activity in the area was small, only independent guerrilla groups, since the Congress had cut off funding of the Contras in the eighties. Many of these resistance fighters would take jobs in Honduras for as much as two years to finance a couple of months of killing Sandinistas in Nicaragua. Then they would start the cycle over again. As a result, they accomplished very little. Particularly not enough to justify the move of political prisoners.

"This prisoner move is significant," Jay insisted to Moe. "And if it does not relate to events at the point of departure, it must relate to the destination. I want a detailed profile on this Rio San Juan Province, ASAP."

"Like yesterday, Boss?" Moe inquired.

"Think that way and get it to me by mid-afternoon."

Colonel Watie barged in without a knock. "I want everything G-Two has on the Gulyakin network."

"There's damn little new," Jay responded.

"I want everything. Turn over all you have from the past, also every little bit and snippet you have developed since Lew Cutler's death."

It turned out to be quite a lot. Somewhat sheepishly, Jay handed over the stack. "I'm, ah, sorry I went off in a half-ass manner on my own and authorized the insertion of Legion intel personnel on the mainland, in direct disobedience to standing orders, Colonel. It's just . . . well, damnit, I wanted to make certain whether or not Gulyakin was involved."

"If I didn't know you would have done that, Jay, you'd never have been confirmed as G-Two. I won't ask what use you planned to make of this stuff. But as of now, your promotion to Lieutenant Colonel is official."

Somewhat mollified, Jay felt encouraged to mention his present puzzler. "I can't put it all together as of now. Why move those prisoners when there's no threat of their imminent release by friendly forces?"

"Why, indeed," Watie responded enigmatically. "Keep after it, Jay. You know, perhaps Ortega is planning a move against Honduras and wants the prisoners far from a possible rescue operation and out of the combat area."

"That could be it. We'll center on that for a while, now you've got something cooking on the Cutler thing."

Taking the large bundle of paperwork, Col. Watie returned to his office and began to pore over it.

Margaret Ainsley-Trowbridge heard the sound like a giant bronze bell echoing inside her head. Muzzily she fought it, until it resolved into the insistent ringing of her doorbell. Her mouth tasted like a compost pit, dry from a layer of lime. Someone had started two furious fires in her eye sockets, and black-cowled monks burned heretics at the stake in her belly. Naked, her hair in frizzy tangles, she lay between two strapping enlisted Legionnaires. The bedroom, like the rest of the house, was in wild disarray, with empty bottles, glasses, and clothing strewn everywhere. The distant clamor continued.

"Shit!" Margaret hissed.

She awakened one Legionnaire by crawling over him. He responded with a not-too-spunky erection. Margaret paused for a fast kiss and a fondling, while she gave the slow-rising phallus a playful tweek. Sighing in exasperation, she broke away for the miles-long trample down the hallway to get a furtive peek through the curtains in the living room. At once she winced and hurried away.

Back in the bedroom she greeted her lean, mean lovers with shushing noises. "It's that old dragon, the big bad Indian brought in to take care of us poor little widows," she warned. "God, how I loathe do-gooders."

"Have her come on in," the roused Legionnaire suggested, waggling his now rigid phallus. "Maybe a little of this will do her good."

"Never waste gourmet food on those who cannot taste," Margaret admonished. Then she brightened. "Fix me a drink, honey. I'm going to give Tom a wakeup like he's never had before."

Licking her lips, Margaret began to fondle the sleeping Legionnaire, her hungry mouth moving closer each moment to his elongating member.

Pastel hues streaked the western sky over the distant mainland. Still troubled by his uninformative intelligence reports, Lt. Col. Jay Solice sat alone at the far end of the bar in the Officers' Mess. Several Cohort officers and their wives occupied the dining room and halfway along the mahogany two young, new, and decidedly nervous ensigns tried out the privileges of rank. It was amusingly obvious to Jay that they would rather be at the Hofbrau, as would he. Yet he wanted to be alone, to mull over the puzzle of Nicaragua.

Like Col. Watie, he remembered the brief invasion of Honduras by Nicaraguan troops in eighty-eight. Everything seemed to point to such an adventure again. Only peripherally did the news impinge on his contemplations. Then, following another of those Bad Taste of the Year raisin commercials, Peter Jennings commanded his full attention.

"Nicaragua is in the news again tonight," the long-faced, light-haired ABC anchor informed his viewers. "And for once, the administration is not taking potshots at that country's government. The reason, unfortunately, is a terrible tragedy. Three nights ago, the undisciplined rabble of a military force calling itself the International Brigade attacked a defenseless mission hospital station near San Carlos, in the remote province of Rio San Juan, Nicaragua. The hospital patients and staff were massacred in a brutal manner. As soon as they learned of the atrocity, Nicaraguan authorities rushed troops and civilian relief workers to the scene this morning. Here's ABC correspondent Trent Jarmon, from the demolished hospital outside San Carlos."

The scene changed and Lt. Col. Solice found himself looking at the bloodied corpses of his misplaced prisoners. It could be no one else. Some still wore the green fatigue trousers issued them when they fought as Contras. Wheels spun and jay turned out a new scenario to account for this unusual turn.

Those prisoners had not been moved there for an elaborate and contrived execution. Not even a devious bastard like Daniel Ortega would cook up a scheme like that. Their deaths were a part of something else. Most likely, Jay now thought, not an invasion of Honduras. Where then? Baby-faced Trent Jarmon soon told him.

"Nicaraguan authorities confirm that the mutinous faction of the International Brigade, an organization much like the American Foreign Legion, has crossed over into Costa Rica and taken refuge in a mountainous region to the southwest of Lake Managua, which forms part of the border between Nicaragua and Costa Rica. They have so far defied Costa Rican government appeals to lay down their arms. This is Trent Jarmon, San Carlos, Rio San Juan Province, Nicaragua." Dumb shits can't get anything right, Jay thought, any high school geography student should know Lake *Nicaragua*, not Managua, lies wholly within the country.

"Since that taped report from the scene of the massacre," Peter Jennings returned to say, "Jarmon was present when President Daniel Ortega made this impassioned appeal."

"I am distraught," the interpreter's voice spoke for Ortega, "over the barbaric murder of these innocents. Among them were fifteen men and women from the United States, who had come here believing in our cause and the further-ance of world peace, only to find brutality and a terrible death. I urge, no, I beg the perpetrators of this horrible crime to lay down their arms and surrender to the author-ities of our neighbor, Costa Rica. I would also remind them that Nicaragua is not without resources. The sanctity of our nation has been defiled, persons under our protection have been killed. We cannot stand by and see this awful deed go unpunished. In the name of human rights, I call on all freedom-loving peoples to rise up and voice their indigna-tion. Then, in the light of world opinion, if these mis-creants are not delivered up for judgment, Nicaragua will be compelled to take what steps are necessary to punish them."

Bingo! Jay's Apache visage lit up with confidence. Nicaragua wasn't going to invade Honduras. They were going after Costa Rica! The Legion was back in business. Jay left the bar for the nearest telephone.

"Get me on to Col. Watie," he requested of the CQ.

"I'm sorry, Colonel, but he's not here. I believe he's takin' Maj. Simmons to dinner."

"Ah, fine. Any idea wher—, er, never mind," Maj. Solice concluded and hung up as the Commandant entered the mess with Maj. Simmons on his arm. Jay hurried to him. "Colonel, I have to speak to you right now and alone," Jay blurted out, which earned him a dirty look from Honey.

"Whatever it is, you can spill it out right here, Jay," Col. Watie responded, somewhat mollifying his date.

Point by point, in brief, hard phrases, Jay laid out his concept of what the recent intelligence, and the news of the massacre actually implied. Watie agreed at once.

"We'll go to my office. Damn, there goes the prime rib I was hankering for."

"I'd like to come along, Norm," Honey appealed. "Why don't I order for us both and bring it in bowser bags?"

"Sounds great," Col. Watie agreed. "But this is a biggie and we've got a lot of catching up to do. You're too beautiful to be hanging over a situations map, when I can ill afford the distraction. You can help, though, by calling Pops and having him meet us at headquarters. Ask him to start calling in the staff, also."

Honey produced a pout, then nodded briskly and went about her task with alacrity. She suspected this would turn out to be an all-night session.

CHAPTER
5

From his comfortable New England saltbox house on Cat Cay, Pops Henderson, the Legion Sergeant Major, contacted the staff in their homes and elsewhere and provided special transportation for all to Corsair Cay. While he did, Cay, Watie called the White House. He interrupted the President at a cocktail reception for European diplomats, prior to a state dinner, honoring the British Prime Minister, a protegé of Margaret Thatcher.

"Is this important?" President Dalton Hunter shaped into the mouthpiece of the scrambler phone.

"You bet it is. Nic——..."

"I know *where*. How long will it take you to get ready?"

"We're on it now. Five days to a polished Ops. Order. But, damnit, that Navy of ours needs another six months to smooth out the kinks. I'd like to know why the Legion got saddled with a prune like O'Fallon."

"You mean why *you* got saddled with the good Admiral," the President chuckled. "Because Tom O'Fallon knows his business and is a darn good teacher. Once he and his training crew pull out, I thought we might reinstitute the rank of Commodore for your Navy, with other suitable changes in rank I think you'll like."

"We can worry about that crap another time. I need to see you tonight."

"I have a state dinner. It'll have to be at eleven, Colonel."

"Twenty-three hundred is fine with me, Mr. President. Right now the Legion has to beat Danny Boy into Costa Rica," Watie said tightly.

"That's where you think it will be, eh? I figured north," Hunter responded, a surprised note in his voice.

"Why fight an army when you can pick on an unarmed nation?" Watie asked rhetorically.

"I suppose if I were Alfred E. Newman, I'd think that way, too," Hunter answered.

"Who?" Watie came back, confused.

"Your Danny Boy, the Alfred E. Newman of Central America. With the U.S. Congress in his hip pocket I'm sure he goes around quite often saying, 'What, me worry?'" Watie joined in the President's laughter. "Get it in high, Norm. I don't want to be caught like Reagan was over Honduras. Let's have the Legion ready at a moment's notice."

It took forty-seven minutes for the staff to assemble in the Headquarters conference room. Watie wasted no time on preliminaries. After naming the suspected target, he began issuing orders.

"Jay, I want you to immediately dispatch the entire Latin American Scout platoon to Honduras. They're to take all the surplus M-Sixteens, special indigenous asset weapons and ammunition you can lay hands on. Sam, aid him in that. The Latino scouts are to train up Miskito Indian refugees and cross into Northeastern Nicaragua at their earliest convenience. Their job will first be to recruit. Arm and train everyone who will sign up, and I mean men, women, and children down to twelve years. In the meantime, Jay, have your Assistant Two scour Legion ranks for as many Indian volunteers as he can round up. Then you are to travel with them, and take command of operations in the designated area."

"Hey, I get a combat command?" Jay enthused.

"Don't get a big head," Watie snapped jokingly. Then he

handed Jay a book. "I want you to organize your strike force on the order of Chesty Puller's famous Company M. Chesty had recognized the superiority of Indian troops back in twenty-seven and kicked hell out of the original Sandinistas with them. I figure Danny Ortega will be a pushover for the same tactics." Watie paused and eyed the rest of the staff. "Mark, Chuck, Mick, I want you to stick around after the meeting for a special chore. Now let's get a look at the maps of our operational areas."

"Areas?" Pat Andrews asked as Pops brought in a large-scale set of maps of Honduras, Nicaragua, and Costa Rica.

"Right, Andy. Look these over carefully, all of you. Starting tomorrow, you are to work up two sets of Operations Plans. One for a strike on Nicaragua, with a special training mission to Costa Rica, and a harassing force to make life difficult for any Sandinista invasion troops. The other plan will be for a straight intervention force, plus a training mission to the Costa Ricans." Watie directed his attention to Chuck Taylor.

"What I mean by a training mission is removal of the entire Legion training establishment from the Cay to Costa Rica."

Despite his years of professional soldiering, Chuck Taylor gaped.

A yawning guard pulled his white-gloved hand from his mouth and saluted smartly as the long, black staff car pulled up to the White House gate. "Good evening, sirs. Are you expected?"

"Colonel Watie and three Legion staff officers," the driver announced.

"Ah, yes, the Liberty Corps. The President is expecting them." He stepped back, saluted, and triggered the electric gate control.

A low fire burned in the fireplace of the Lincoln Study, where the President greeted his guests. He urged them to comfortable chairs and took their orders for drinks. Watie had coffee, the others iced tea. The moment the White

House butler departed, Watie jumped into the middle of things.

"We're already moving, Mr. President. By tomorrow evening we'll have fifty of our Spanish-speaking scouts in Honduras, to organize the Miskito Indians as a G-force. Once in-country, the Miskitos'll rally their fellow tribesmen. Our Spanish speakers can concentrate on the local population, and before long, Ortega will have more trouble than he can handle."

Dalton Hunter frowned. "I'm not so certain that's such a good idea at this time."

"What's the matter with it, sir? We've *got* to make this strike into Nicaragua, to force the Sandinistas to realize that starting wars can be painful. Hell, I suggest you have the Company start up the Contras again. The more trouble we can stir up in Ortega's backyard, the less time and troops he'll have to play bully with in another country. Outside of not having an army, the major thing that makes Costa Rica attractive for an invasion is the ease with which Sandinista supplies can be moved on Lake Nicaragua from the very heart of the industrialized area to the border of the victims."

"I realize that. Yet, I still have to deal with Congress," the President sighed.

"Another telling point, Mr. President. And it works two ways. If we operate solely in Costa Rica, and manage to push the Sandinistas back, the moment they're driven across their own frontier, the stinking liberals in Congress will force the Legion to withdraw, even if they have to use U.N. intervention to do it. To them, it's simply unthinkable for the communists to suffer a defeat anywhere in the world, and particularly in Central America. But if we're already kicking ass deep inside Nicaragua and have the hearts and minds of the people behind us, to say nothing of their armed support, there's a good chance of catching Ortega between two fronts and smashing his Sandinista power for all time." Watie paused for breath, and to marshal his thoughts.

"By the same token, if the Legion is limited to a blocking action, and can't even pursue the Sandinistas into Nicaragua, the price we'll pay in lives will be horrendous. Also, our supply lines will be unacceptably long for a war of attrition. The jackals of the media would start hooting about 'another Vietnam,' and this time, damnit, they'd be right."

Worried about initiating an invasion on the eve of an election, Hunter lacked the decisiveness that had marked his two brilliant terms. "There's a lot at stake, outside of Nicaragua," Hunter began hesitantly.

"Hell, yes," Watie barked, his ire rising. "All of Central America."

"There's the election, also," Hunter reminded him. "I'd like to hold off on this until I've had a chance to discuss it with my running mate."

"Ollie'd go for it, you damn bet he would," Watie blurted. "Uh, excuse me, Mr. President. That was tactless."

"I appreciate your anxiety, Norm. I'd like to personally wring that Ortega's neck. The people out at Langley came up with the same decision Col. Solice put forward. Those killed in the so-called massacre were not hospital patients. At least not all of them. They were the prisoners in a forced labor battalion. Any odds on whether there are mutineers out there?"

"I'll give even odds the bullets and grenades at San Carlos came from Sandinista rifles," Watie stated flatly.

"There was an American physician among the victims. A, ah, Doctor Herman Silberman. They never found all of him."

"How do you mean that, Mr. President?"

"It seems there was a crocodile involved. In spite of that and all you've said, let's let this hang fire for twenty-four hours. I'll get back to you with an answer by then."

Ordinarily a man of infinite patience, Arkady Gulyakin found himself becoming restive. His anxiety rose from his own success, which had ensured for him a long and relatively safe sinecure in demolishing the Legion from inside. Yet he found his temper flaring, forbearance flagging.

Great things were happening in Central America. Yet *he*

had to attend an antique auction to keep up his ridiculous cover. *Pohvozmo Lenina yaeechkat!* By the testicles of Lenin, he thought again in English. It seemed ludicrous to maintain a false identity when every one in the country who mattered knew who he was anyway. At least he had been able to release some of his tensions this evening.

Arkady reached over and patted the small, round, peaches-and-cream fanny of the pretty young girl beside him in the king-size waterbed. The prudish, old-maid mentality of Soviet society, he thought scornfully. Such liaisons were scrupulously forbidden. What a pity, when there were thousands of sweet young things in Mother Russia, every bit as sexually athletic as little Linda.

The daughter of a trustworthy liberal senator, Linda had grown up in an open, or free, lifestyle, as the decadent Americans called it. By what she had told Arkady, she had enthusiastically surrendered her virtue seven years ago, at the tender age of eight, to a junior-high boy of thirteen, whose family lived at the nudist park Linda frequented with the family of a friend. She had certainly satisfied Arkady's fastidious appetites. Visualizing their strenuous coupling caused a stirring in Gulyakin's loins. Arousal came rapidly. Scooted closer, he rubbed his rigid member along the curve of her buttock and received the desired response.

"Ooooh," Linda cooed, rising on one elbow, blinking big, cobalt eyes. "Daddy's ready again." Swiftly she went down on hands and knees. "Let's go doggie style this time, Daddy," Linda pleaded.

Grinning like a boy with his first conquest, Arkady positioned himself and thrust between her widespread thighs, still half-inclined to skip tomorrow's auction.

CHAPTER
6

Braying traffic made a steady racket over the Potomac basin as Lt. Col. Mark Kelly checked his watch and stepped from the cab at 3600 New York Avenue, N.E., in Washington, D.C. The time was precisely 0830. He entered the building and went directly to the small cubbyhole office of Scott Nelson. Of all the staff of the *Washington Times*, Scott was the most sympathetic to the Legion. Mark had met Scott in the Army and they had continued their friendship in the years afterward. The reporter, in shirtsleeves, greeted his visitor and waved to a chair.

"Clear that crap off and park yourself. What's this important story, Mark?"

Lt. Col. Kelly removed a stack of used tractor paper from the chair and eased into it. "One that I judge will knock your socks off."

Amid the usual clutter of open files, stacks of old copy, a dictionary, and a style book, rested a computer terminal and keyboard. Scott cleared the screen and nodded to Mark.

"Shoot. I'll key it in while you tell me about it."

"This goes back a ways. Actually to the beginning of the Legion. Do you remember when Gator Gantry apparently went berserk and began shooting people in the D.C. sub-

way? He was supposed to have accidentally fallen under
the wheels of a train. Not long after that Lew Cutler got
into a running shoot-out on the Beltway. The local police
and the FBI sort of swept those incidents under the rug.
Both were attempts at murder. In Gantry's case, they suc-
ceeded. Since that time there have been several persons
apprehended on Corsair Cay involved in espionage or sab-
otage. I'll go into that later. First I want to introduce the
key player.

"There's a man in this country, living in Savannah,
Georgia, by the name of Arkady Gulyakin. He is, to the
best of our intelligence efforts, a major in the *Mokkryee
Della*—Wet Affairs—section of the *Komitet Gosudarstvennoi Bezopasnosti*—the KGB. He's known internation-
ally as the Ice Man."

"Wow!" Scott remarked laconically. "That sounds like
it's straight out of adventure fiction. You know, James
Bond, or Mac Bolan, all that stuff. Or an article in *New
Breed* magazine."

"It's real enough, Scotty, believe me. Apparently Gulyakin is directing all Soviet efforts against the Legion. Following the planting of two female agents on the Cay, and
an attempt to poison the Legion water supply, our intelligence people interrogated the agents involved and developed the Gulyakin connection. We turned all of this over to
the FBI. They in turn refused to accept the results of our
investigation, placed Gulyakin under loose surveillance
and ignored the whole matter. Since then we have lost
eleven killed, three seriously injured, with a million dollars
worth of equipment destroyed when a barge exploded. The
cause of the destruction was a cover raid by Spetznats
troops, under direction of Gulyakin. The man who triggered the blast was apprehended and interrogated. We've
also had the departure of a female Soviet agent who had
penetrated the Legion as a recruit." Mark paused again and
let Scott catch up. His next words came out colored by
anger.

"When we took *that* to the FBI, they chuckled politely
and patted us on our heads like good little boys. It was,
they said, the product of overactive imaginations. Then,

somehow, Gulyakin engineered the construction of a lamp-post bomb, which killed our Regular Army liaison and his wife. The FBI called it a random act of protest against the military by person or persons unknown. We traced it back to Gulyakin."

"That's one hell of a story, Mark. What do you want me to do with it?"

"Print it," Lt. Col. Kelly bit off.

"The, ah, Bureau might get a little salty about that. To say nothing of your KGB boy, Gulyakin."

"Fuck the Bureau," Kelly said nastily. "As to Gulyakin . . . as of oh-eight-thirty this morning, he has been in Legion hands."

Finishing his morning tea, Arkady Gulyakin wiped his lips and glanced at the wall clock. Noting the time as 0843, he stretched luxuriously and pushed back from the dining room table. His driver had taken the energetic Linda back to the dormitory of her private school two hours earlier. Even so, Arkady still felt the flow and pleasant tingle generated by their night of wild abandon. With the grace of a cat, the tall, muscular agent rose and went into the hallway. There he put on his hat and coat. Like it or not, it was time to go play his little role. Two bodyguards trailed him to the door.

"I'll be back by fourteen hundred hours, Fyeodor," he informed his second in command.

Arkady Gulyakin directed his driver to take the long way to the center city auction house. He deliberately stalled for the sheer pleasure of delaying a dreaded task, a most unusual extravagance, but one to which he felt entitled after his success with Lew Cutler. Rush hour traffic had thinned by the time Gulyakin reached the heart of town.

"Go get this serviced and be back by thirteen-forty," Gulyakin ordered his driver.

He and his watchdogs arrived at the auction in the middle of the sale and Gulyakin settled into the routine of bidding on preselected items. The smallest flick of his numbered card was all it took to signal an offer. In a short while he had picked up two antebellum side desks and a

quality leaded glass sideboard. Fully into the rhythm of the
contest between buyers, Arkady began to enjoy himself.

Suddenly a huge hand wrapped around his neck and he
was lifted off his feet. Arkady made harsh, strangled
sounds and kicked his feet ineffectually. To add to his
panic, glances to the sides showed both bodyguards effectively neutralized. The KGB agent recognized a Legion
major, Mick Orenda, and the tall, handsome Lt. Col.
Chuck Taylor. Voices broke into a disturbed murmur and
several persons attempted to rise.

With little effort, the three Legionnaires hustled their
captives out of the auction and into a waiting rental car.
"Take us on to the mole," Watie told Orenda.

Although crowded, the rented station wagon provided
adequate transportation. The KGB noncoms made no effort
to hamper the operation. When Gulyakin began to babble
protests, Watie shut him up with another squeeze of his
ham hand. At an isolated spot on the breakwater, Mick
stopped the car and everyone got out. Riot cuffs rendered
the bodyguards helpless. Gulyakin stared in appreciation at
the impressive appearance of a 42-foot Nemesis boat,
grounded on the sand below the riprap of broken concrete.
Exercising little care for the prisoners' safety, the Legion
raiding party ushered them aboard. The diesels rumbled
and the Arnesen surface drive performed its magic. The
helmsman set a course for Corsair Cay.

Arkady Gulyakin demonstrated considerable cool in his
first, and to him disastrous, face-to-face meeting with Norman Stand Watie. While the powerful boat came up to
speed, he glanced around in grudging admiration.

"This is quite a vessel you have here, Col. Watie. You
wouldn't consider selling a few to the Soviet Union would
you?"

Watie made a face that might accompany tasting bad
fish. "Gag him," he growled.

For all of being "one of them," Lt. Cato Padilla had so
far received a cool reception in Honduras. Traveling in

mufti, he and his platoon of 49 men were met at the El
Dulce Nombre airport by a Captain Juan Pablo Gomez of
the Ejercito de Honduras, the Army Service branch of the
Fuerzas Armadas de Honduras. Like his Legion counterpart, Capt. Gomez was endowed with strong Indian features. Reluctantly the Honduran officer agreed to transport
the Legionnaires to one of the Miskito refugee camps.

"Certainly you can go, Teniente, but don't be surprised
at what you find. These people have suffered for so long as
their memories go back. First the revolutions, then the Somoza government policies, then the new war and the bas-
tardo comunismos under Ortega. They know only poverty,
displacement, and death. They are suspicious of everyone."

In the truck, on the way, Gomez continued the theme.
"Their most recent history is the cause of almost breaking
them apart as a people. The Sandinistas conducted a determined war of extermination against them. The world press
ignored them. They had their homes in places far from the
centers of importance and news. Also, who cared they
were being butchered? They were only indios, no? Then,
when your country got a good president in, and aid was
sent to the Contras, the Miskitos got the short end again.
As I said, their area of operation was too far from locales
that would generate headlines.

"Unfortunately, they were also the only ones in a position to establish a firm base of operations in-country, since
they had nearly a hundred percent indigenous support."
Gomez paused in his lecture, then swore bitingly when a
front wheel hit a deep pothole. "Right now they need food,
medical supplies, and clothing far more than guns and ammunition. There is an organization of Americans providing
this, Angel something-or-other, but in limited quantities
and only once or twice a year.

"The tragedy is that these Americanos are Marxist pro-
pagandists, and along with their supplies they bring tales to
the Miskitos of how wonderful it is to live under the Sandinista regime. Much to my anger, and disgust, a few have

listened. They crossed back and were never heard from again."

"Isn't there another relief organization? One that's backed by *SOF* magazine?" Padilla asked.

"Yes. But alas, they haven't the finances and organization behind them that the followers of Marx seem to possess. Also the Sandinistas have shot down some of their airplanes. The Sandinistas call them brigands and pirates, as does your Congress and the media."

"Let's get one thing straight from the beginning," Padilla insisted. "We in the Legion are stateless people. My folks may have been born in Texas, but like our Legion motto says, the Legion is our fatherland. You can bet there's no love lost between the Legion and the U.S. Congress."

When they reached the camp, Cato could not wipe the shock and misery from his face. The Miskitos lived in grueling poverty that made the tar-paper *barrios* of Mexican border towns look like mansions. Some had only a ragged tarp, strung between three or four trees, for a shelter. Nearly all of the children ran around naked, all were barefoot. Bellies swollen by malnutrition and vitamin deficiency were as common as flies and other insects. At once he ordered his medics to treat the worst cases and at least concoct placebos for the rest. Their LST load of initial supplies was not due to pass between the Caribbean seacoast twin villages of Barra and Caratasca and to dock at Puerto Lempira for a week.

In light of this, Cato took up a collection that afternoon among his platoon, and hit the Honduran soldiers as well. He selected one of his medical cross-trained men to accompany Gomez back to El Dulce Nombre later in the day, with instructions to purchase what he could to create a crude dispensary. He then set his clerk to drafting a list of supplies to be flown in on an emergency basis. Heading the list, Lt. Padilla insisted, were a medical team, a field hospital, antibiotics, and dietary supplements.

"They'll need uniforms, boots, and some cash as well," he insisted before walking away with Capt. Gomez.

From the material contained in the Ops. Order, Padilla

had learned about the YATAMA resistance fighters. With the medical situation underway, he inquired about them from Gomez.

Capt. Gomez answered him with a satisfied smirk. "I doubt very much that YATAMA will allow your Legion to operate in the area."

That made no sense at all to Cato Padilla. "Why not? Hell, they've been fighting the Sandinistas for twenty years with no outside support at all, other than the isolated patches of jungle land on which your government has allowed them to establish camps. I'd think they would be ripe for all the aid we can bring them."

"You are only too correct, Teniente Padilla. They are an independent lot, proud, too. Perhaps too much so to accept help. No one, at least in the Ejercito, knows exactly who the YATAMA are. I'll introduce you to some resistance fighters who have recently returned from an armed visit to friends and relatives on the Nicaraguan side. Note their attitudes, multiply the reactions by four, and you'll have a fair idea of the YATAMA position."

Lt. Cato Padilla eyed the barefoot, ragtag crew of resistance fighters with a jaundiced eye, albeit with pity in his heart. He listened to their accounts of conditions in Daniel Ortega's workers' paradise with growing anger. The casual manner of mentioning that this family or that had been murdered down to the last small child, chilled him. True to his role as a great humanitarian, Ortega wanted the land for good communists, so the Indians had to go. After all, as the eldest of the fighting men said of the Marxist dictator, to Ortega it wasn't as though his troops were killing people.

"Did you see any Americans there? Yanquis?" Padilla asked.

"Oh, yes, several. At least three bands of them. They smiled and passed out medical supplies during the day. Then, at night, one of them called in the Sandinista soldiers to kill our Miskitos. Maybe one, two of them did this, I don't think the others knew about it. This happened three times. We escaped by fighting."

Fury and shame led Lt. Padilla onto shaky ground. "If you could point out the traitors, I would personally lead a team of my men to terminate them."

The old man shrugged. "They are like the smoke. It rises and the wind blows it away. Today these two-faced ones are in the jungle. Tomorrow, they drink beer in Managua and tell how wonderful the Sandinistas are."

Bitterness coloring his rampant emotions, Lt. Padilla held a cursory inspection of the camp, then called a council of war. "First we take care of the living conditions," he informed his men. "Then we start kicking ass on the Sandinistas."

Believing that he had somewhat swayed Capt. Gomez's negative opinion of their operation, Lt. Padilla went to him early the next afternoon after the Honduran officer and Cato's sergeant had returned with medicine, fresh eggs, and shovels.

"Captain, I'd like permission to move the entire encampment to higher ground. These people need to be away from that sluggish creek. It only serves as an incubator for mosquitoes and other insects. Sanitation is wretched and the ground too damp for proper housing."

Gomez eyed the Legion officer, one eyebrow cocked in a dubious manner. His response came hesitantly. "The current camp is on land, ah, designated by my government for the refugees. There is no disputing that. But that hill? *Quién sabe?* One is wise not to rock *el barqo*, no?"

Catching the direction of the Honduran's circumlocutions, Cato made a slightly different approach. "Yet, it is tactically wise for troops to occupy the high ground, am I right? Well then, would it be acceptable for me to set up our camp on that hill?"

A beatific smile wriggled Gomez's flourishing mustache. He caught the idea quickly and knew that the refugee camp would not only gravitate up to where its benefactors had settled, but would soon be armed as well. For the first time he extended a friendly gesture by placing a hand on Padilla's shoulder.

"You are a brilliant soldier, Teniente Padilla. Also somewhat of a diplomat. I see nothing prohibiting your establishing a camp there. Once that is accomplished, can we get down to that selecting and training of men to do as you said? Attacking those *hijos de chingada* Sandinistas?"

CHAPTER
7

With a banshee screech and the rushing surge of a locomotive, the big shell rippled overhead, to land in a splash and a horrendous explosion some three hundred yards beyond the streamlined powerboat. Even the gulls had cleared the area. Fifteen men, more foolhardy than the birds, wearing their dark blue nylon windbreakers with the big yellow letters on the back and matching baseball caps, crouched in the commodious open cockpit. Several of them seemed as if they were about to die of sheer terror. They clutched their M-16s in white-knuckled grips.

"Jesus Christ! *Nobody* makes artillery with that range," a freckle-faced younger man declared.

"They didn't drop it out of the sky at us, Junior," an older agent riposted.

"Oh, yeah? Look at that weird thing shadowing us," the youthful FBI man countered, pointing above and behind the throttled-down boat.

"There's two more of them," the man at the helm announced.

"Ahoy the boat," the tinny voice over the bullhorn blared at them. "Stand clear of Corsair Cay or you will be boarded and sunk."

Braver than his fellows, one middle-aged agent snatched

up their loud-hailer. "This is the FBI. We are here on legitimate Bureau business. We have warrants for the arrest of one Norman Stand Watie and two John Does, for kidnapping, illegal transportation across state lines, and violation of diplomatic immunity. We're coming ashore to serve them."

"If that boat moves in any direction other than away, I've got orders to put a Javelin missile up your ass," came the reply.

"You can't do that. We're the FBI." That got a Bronx cheer.

"Get clear of restricted waters or we'll open fire," another pilot's voice joined in.

"We're operating on the Director's personal authority," the courageous agent growled.

"Then you'd better get on the radio and call him up to find out what a terrible mistake you've made," the first pilot taunted.

"M-maybe we ought to call the Director," an older agent suggested.

"And give in to these mercenary slobs?" the agent with the bullhorn sneered. Then he studied the bristling stores pods on the Merlins. "I, ah, suppose it wouldn't hurt."

The Director of the FBI came on immediately. "Where are you and what's going on?"

"W-we're seven miles off Corsair Cay, sir. Attempting to serve the warrants on Watie and the Does."

"Well?" the Director's harsh tones carried over the radio.

"We've been ordered to desist by armed aircraft and were told to contact you."

"Perhaps that's a good thing. I want you to turn around and get out of there."

"Are you sure, sir? They fired an artillery piece at us," the bellicose agent countered.

"If they fired *at* you, they would have hit you. There's been a, ah, change of considerable magnitude. It severely affects the Bureau."

"How's that, sir?"

"It seems," the Director answered, reluctant to spell it out, "that the *Washington Times* hit the streets about an

hour ago with an extra. It blew the cover off the Gulyakin
espionage case, and said some terrible things about the
Bureau. It even went so far as to claim we refused to arrest
the gentleman in question. Now, if we were to arrest a man
with so popular an image as the Legion Commandant, I
don't think it would prove to be too good an idea." His
voice came over somewhat garbled, it being difficult to
talk while eating crow.

A red light came on atop the camera directly in front of
Col. Norman Stand Watie. At the same time, the floor director in the Legion television station on Corsair Cay
swung his arm down, index finger pointing at the Commandant. Watie folded his hands on the prop desk and
looked directly into the lens.

"Good afternoon," he began, voice a bit rusty. He *hated*
the idea of taking anything off a TelePrompTer. "I am Colonel Norman Stand Watie of the American Foreign Legion.
By now, most of you watching me have already learned
part of the story regarding a Soviet spy ring, the Legion,
and the FBI. It is unfortunate that a certain major newspaper chose to release the story precipitously. Particularly
when it did not have all the facts. As a result, I felt it
necessary to clarify the situation, within the limits imposed
by our Judge Advocate's office—the, ah, Legion attor-
neys, if you will.

"Essentially what appeared in the *Times* article is correct. For over a year now, the FBI has had in its possession
evidence, testimony, and documents sufficient to obtain an
indictment for espionage against Major Arkady Gulyakin
of the KGB, Captain Fyeodor Dobredyn, and other
members of his apparat. Since the FBI has no jurisdiction
on Corsair Cay, that evidence was gathered by the Legion,
and not the FBI. As a result, the Bureau has refused to
implement action against a known Soviet agent. Additional
proof of Major Gulyakin's activities was turned over to the
Bureau, as it developed, and still they refrained from taking him into custody. The last act Major Gulyakin and his
apparat is alleged to have committed is the assassination of
the Regular Army liaison officer to the Legion, Col. Lewis

Cutler, and a number of civilian and military personnel. Still the Bureau refuses to move. It has come to the point where it appears that the Federal Bureau of Investigation is in fact harboring a KGB Wet Affairs operative with a predilection for murdering Legionnaires.

"I, as Legion Commander, have been forced to act in defense of the lives of my men and myself. Because what has been done is technically illegal, I could neither order my men to bring in Major Gulyakin, nor allow them to do so by looking the other way. Therefore, I led the operation to apprehend Major Gulyakin, using volunteers who were fully aware of possible consequences. The Legion will try Major Gulyakin by military court, and execute sentence. Further attemps by the FBI to interfere with the swift course of Justice on behalf of Major Gulyakin will have to be considered willful hostile acts by Soviet surrogates, and treated accordingly. Further information regarding this matter will be made available as they develop, and the trial will be televised. Thank you, and good day."

When the lights went out, Col. Watie stepped from behind the small desk and scrubbed sweat from his brow. "You know, Mark," he confided to Lt. Col. Mark Kelly, "I'm not sure we'll be able to carry this off. But if a Legion tribunal brings in a guilty verdict, I'll personally blow off Gulyakin's head."

"In summation," Dan Rather began, flashing his boyish smile, which belied the graying of his hair, "Corsair Cay has been notorious for pirates for three centuries. It is small wonder that a powerful, well-armed force of international brigands would take it unto themselves to violate the laws of every civilized nation. This foreign gentleman, Mr. Gulyakin, has not been accused of any crime by responsible authorities. Quite to the contrary. He is a guest in our country, a businessman of fine reputation. Yet he is seized and kidnapped off to Corsair Cay on the whim of the leader of a ruthless band of mercenaries, much like the mutinous units of the International Brigade in Central America. And one can't help but wonder if the Butchers of San Carlos looked to Corsair Cay for their example." Rather paused to impress everyone with his No. 3, "would-I-lie-to-you" expression, then launched into the next story.

"Trouble still remains rife in Central America. So far the government of Costa Rica has done nothing to disarm and arrest, or turn back to Nicaragua the mutineers of the International Brigade. Each day more reports are filed of atrocities committed against the peaceful people of Nicaragua and northeastern Costa Rica. A Nicaraguan resolution was introduced in the U.N. today, declaring it a deliberate criminal act for the Costa Rican government to allow an armed and hostile force to exist on the border of a friendly nation. A joint congressional committee, led by Senators Edward Halloran of Connecticut and Kennedy of Massachusetts, and Congressmen Blum of New York and Hayden of California, urged U.S. support of the resolution. Late yesterday afternoon, a Nicaraguan convoy was ambushed inside Nicaragua and Sheldon Shapp was there to cover it."

Footage rolled, showing a disjointed string of American-made army trucks, blasted and still smoldering. The voice-over narration identified the vehicles as belonging to a company of the Sandinista army, bringing supplies to forward elements who sought to make contact with the rebels. Far from the presupposed reaction, it generated an outburst from Lt. Charley Smith at the Hofbrau of Corsair Cay.

"Hey, those are American-made trucks. The Reds got rid of most of them ten years ago. The bastards must have raided every junkyard in the country to come up with that many antiques. Who the hell do they think they're kidding? Look. Look there. That's the only Zil in the whole mess and its caved-in front end is rusty for God's sake."

"Surely those honest folks inNicaragua wouldn't fake a thing like that, Charley," a sarcastic voice answered him.

"Yeah, those news guys could see that, too, couldn't they?" another Legionnaire observed with a snicker. "They'd never go along with something phony."

The graying-haired Vietnam vet cocked his head and eyed the jester askance. "Does a bear shit in the woods? Y'ask me, they prob'ly helped set it up. And we've got Hanoi Jane's commie husband pushing for the U.S. to back

that Nicaraguan resolution. Next thing you know that traitor bitch will start street demonstrations."

Rather's voice intruded again. "President Daniel Ortega
will broadcast a half-hour appeal to the American people
on a CBS special which will replace regular programming
at the end of this evening's news."

"Anybody wanna bet that Danny Boy Ortega'll not remind the audience that the *only* armed force in Costa Rica
is this International Brigade, any more than CBS has?"
Charlie invited sarcastically. "If those Costa Rican guys
were smart, they'd ask for help from the Legion before it's
too damn late."

Without fanfare, President Dalton Hunter arrived on
Corsair Cay at 0200 hours for a secret conference with Col.
Norman Watie and his staff. He greeted the Legion officers
with a blooming smile and radiated much of his old
strength and spirit.

"Oliver has agreed that a strike into Nicaragua is the
only sensible way to stop any invasion of Costa Rica. The
way he put it was, 'Twenty years ago I'd have probably
said nuke the bastards until they glow.' He accepts the political necessity of no direct involvement, and asked me to
wish you good luck and a successful campaign from him."

"That's a relief," Watie stated frankly. "Your twenty-four
hours grew enough I almost gave the green light without a
release."

"You wouldn't do that, Norm," the President chided
gently.

"I got Gulyakin, didn't I?" Watie cracked back.

Hunter frowned. "Which brings up another matter I
came here for. You can forget about trying Arkady Gulyakin. For once, the people are against you on this. They
have a strong sense of justice, and they're accustomed to
seeing that done through the regular courts. Given the
media hyperbole about denying the poor man his civil
rights . . ."

Uncharacteristically, Watie interrupted the President.
"Fuck the media. They and Gulyakin work for the same
people. We have the proof, the *proof*, that Gulyakin set up

the murder of Lew and T.J., and was responsible for all that went on around here. Now I'm supposed to turn him over to some bureaucratic faggot who will set him up in some comfy resort and feed him caviar until his government can arrange to transport him home and reward him for a job well done. The whole idea disgusts me." Panting, Watie remained on his feet, head down, swaying from side to side like an exhausted bull.

His voice distorted by anger at Watie's outburst and sympathy for his reason, Dalton Hunter spoke tightly. "It would have been better if you had set up an ambush and blown away that KGB scumbag, then said nothing to anyone about it. As it is, I'm forced to do this. Gulyakin and company are to be delivered up for arrest by the FBI at Dulles Airport the moment the Legion can bring them there. In return, I will personally force the Director of the Bureau to not only drop all kidnapping charges, but admit FBI culpability in forcing the Legion to defend itself by denying due process. Those responsible in the local office will be forced to resign."

"Unnh," Watie grunted. "And for what? Gulyakin will probably be exchanged next chance the Soviets get."

A pained expression crossed the President's face. "The, ah, Soviet internal security division of the KGB has already arrested five American students of a cultural exchange group on trumped-up charges of espionage in Moscow. It seems, ah, entirely likely they will bring forward such a proposal."

"It seems I've heard that song before," Watie sang in a fractured, off-key tone. "I'll do it. Because you want it that way. But, other than being alive, I won't guarantee the emotional condition of the prisoner when he's turned over. I want it made clear to him and his superiors what I'll be doing to his colleagues in Central America."

CHAPTER
8

With all the bustle of white cells in an infected blood-stream, Corsair Cay came alive at 0615 on Wednesday morning. During the night, "Old Patches," the *Alexander M. Patch*, AP-122, and the *Meteor*, T-AKR-9, slid silently into Corsair Cove and tied up in loading position. Great doors opened wide, they now took aboard long lines of Legionnaires and their equipment. First aboard the ships were the entire Legion training staff and their equipment, plus First Cohort, with the entire roster of Legion support Centuries. Ten miles offshore the first Legion Carrier Task Force steamed patterns in the Atlantic, running antiaircraft drills with their own supersonic Harriers simulating enemy fast movers. To add to the discomfort of those aboard, the Legion fast-attack boats made practice runs on them. In the sheltered, lee side of the cove, the Merlins got a workout also, prior to departure.

"Toltec Zero-zero, another shot like that and you'll stove in my bow," the commander of one 63-foot Harley growled.

Above, and slightly abaft of, him Capt. Jim Levin sweated blood. It all looked so damned easy, *watching* it. "Rog, ah, Gaul. D'you want another forward approach? Over."

"Right. Only this time, don't begin your final descent until we've matched velocities."

"Rog." Well shit, Arizona Jim thought, stung by the remark. Any kid would know that. Apparently *this* kid didn't, he acknowledged upon honest reflection.

Nothing for it but to try again. Arizona Jim increased the throttles and the Merlin leaped ahead of the slowly maneuvering Harley 64. Off to his right he saw a swarm of activity as the South African G6 155 guns were registered on offshore dyemarker targets. Palms damp, he rotated the agile bird and lined up for a straight-in approach. Perfect . . . perfect . . . *damn*! The coxswain of the 64 jinked the boat to the left. Jim compensated by a slight movement to his right. Dead center. Cut back on the throttle, let it come to the preselected point. Easy. Crossing the bow. Markers centered, port and starboard. Speed matched. Hover mode. Descend. Power back . . . back . . . *Ta-whump*!

Arizona Jim groaned. Would he ever get it right?

"That's a lot better, Toltec Zero-zero. You didn't even oilcan the deck," came the dry voice of the ensign commanding the boat.

Punk kid, Jim thought uncharitably. Fresh out of the Officer Advancement Course and bossing a fighting boat like an old salt. "Ready for lift," he responded meekly into the thin boom mike at his lips.

Much like a control tower at an airport, the tall shaft that rose above the warehouses and sheds of the dock area of Corsair Cay gave a commanding view of the surrounding activity. The blue-tinted, outward-slanting glass of the observation and operations platform provided 360-degree coverage. Overlooking all the activity in the cove, and ashore, Col. Norman Stand Watie stood at a small desk, the handset of a secured scrambler telephone in his left hand. The slightly distorted voice of President Dalton Hunter rattled in his ear.

"The Costa Rican Minister Plenipotentiary is here and negotiations are under way, Norm. We're sort of shoehorning this one in, so timing is critical. I want the first elements of the Legion standing by off Puerto Limon and a formal request for intervention in hand before I warn Alf Newman that a Nicaraguan invasion will be met by the Liberty Corps."

"The two transport ships are on schedule for a midnight sailing, Mr. President," Watie assured him. "McDade and the Carrier Task Force will follow in forty-eight hours. What about Congress and the media?"

The stocky, barrel-chested leader of the Free World chuckled softly. "Remember Grenada? Those we can trust in both camps have been advised to stand by for a special presidential announcement. The rest . . . they'll be told when the time's right."

"In other words, the Russians won't know about this twenty-four hours before we do? Good."

"Uh, Norm, we've been receiving satellite pics that show heavy traffic on Lake Nicaragua and a large armored force near San Carlos."

"That's exactly what I expected," Watie answered easily. "What concerns me most is whether Costa Rica will buy the Legion's terms."

"That does seem to be a major stumbling block. Though you needn't worry overly much, with Sam Seagraves and Walt Hayward on the bargaining panel."

"Then I'll leave it in your hands, sir. We've a lot of juggling to do around here," Col. Watie summed up.

"Good enough, Norm," the President responded. "Give Alfie something to worry about, eh?"

Wiping sweat from her forehead, Major Honey Simmons had completed her task of sorting through an endless line of native patients. "I've never been so worn out before," she admitted to the young MD standing beside her. "Not even in Vietnam. And we're only five days in-country. Whoever contrived to stand aside and let these people contract so many diseases, parasites, and injuries ought to be stood against a wall and shot."

Twenty varieties of insects buzzed and hummed around them. The sweet-sour cloy of rotting vegetation and renewing growth, familiar to any jungle, made the humid Honduran air thick and syrupy. Bird voices, squawking and calling, blended with human sounds. Monkeys made rich contributions to the noise level. Barefoot, naked, and nearly naked, brown-skinned people continued to shuffle up to the examination table. Hammers and saws, bulldozers and shovels blended in a profusion of work on the refugee camp digging in on the hillside.

"*Andar alla*," Honey instructed, looking at a suppurating fungus infestation on a child's forearm.

They had specialists for nearly everything, but a shortage of ear, nose, and throat people. Just breathing the air in these parts, Honey had discovered, could get green things growing deep inside a person. Sharp, odd-sounding commands in the Miskito Indian dialect reached her ears from a group of men in new cammo and boots who trained with weapons strange to them. The noxious odor of human excrement, rotting garbage, and animal entrails nearly gagged her when the indifferent breeze shifted a couple of points. She hoped the men digging rifle pits nearby would soon be shifted to the detail working on sanitation facilities.

"*Bueno*, Pepe," she told a big-eyed seven-year-old. "That has grown much smaller. By tomorrow you won't need any more treatment." Honey traced a circle around the inch-wide ring of new, pink flesh that surrounded a spiral fungus much like a ringworm on the little boy's rounded belly. "Go over there. Hanrahan," she yelled to the Legion medic at a table on her left. "Another dose of mercuric oxide ointment for Pepe."

A new sound began to impinge on her consciousness and Honey kept a half-wary eye on a convoy of military trucks that appeared out of the jungle screen and wound around the base of the hill to the old camp, then altered course and started toward the rough road carved into the side of the slope. In the lead, a truck with a blade affixed to the front created yet more improvements in the sparse track. She recognized the Honduran army markings and a chill touched her heart.

Oh, God, was the Honduran army coming to move these poor people back down into that pest hole they'd so recently left? Honey recalled the moving scene on the day they had arrived. She and her team had come in on a convoy escorted by Capt. Gomez of the Honduran army. He had seemed cynical and unfeeling to Honey, yet his eyes showed real hurt when he viewed the shy, frightened, suffering people. Immediately they had begun to set up a hospital, along with distribution points for food and clothing and a recruiting station for the new infiltration force. That, too, had to be, Honey acknowledged. A day passed with no customers.

Her experiences in 'Nam had taught Honey not to despair. When the Indians became sure of their welcome, they followed willingly enough, first to receive food and medical treatment, then to begin building new huts on high, dry ground. Honey was well aware that the move was unauthorized. Now the chances could have caught up with them, just when solid progress had begun to show.

"Good afternoon, Major."

Honey jumped as though stung, then recognized the voice of the Legion's Lt. Cato Padilla. She all but hugged him, realizing from his cheerful demeanor that the convoy must be Legion reinforcements. Immediately she voiced her fears. Cato chuckled tolerantly.

"No, I reckon the Honduras politicos will leave us alone here. With this latest shipment, the camp is completely armed now. No hairsplitting army officer will bother us unless ordered to do so from *very* high up. And no matter how high up, politicians are terrified of people who are armed and able to protect themselves."

Grinding gears over the last steep grade, the trucks arrived. Lt. Col. Jay Solice stepped out to formally take command. "It's nice to be here," Jay declared quietly, rubbing his hands as though washing them.

Clusters of small boys began to whisper and giggle, pointing at Jay's obvious Indian features. Some of the adults were as big-eyed as their youngsters. An *indio* in command? He must be a mighty warrior, the remarks went around.

"First off, I need a place for my troops to rest and get a good meal. Then I need enough native scouts and interpreters in good health to lead the first incursion. We jump off at oh-four-hundred hours."

Startled by this, Cato had expected Jay to command from the base camp, while he, Cato, led the troops in the field. Cato Padilla stammered out his question: "Y-you mean that soon? An—and you're going to take them out?"

"Of course," Jay said lightly. Then he read the spirit behind the questions. "You'll get your chance, Lieutenant. Provided all goes well, you'll be heading up all the covert ops over the border into Nicaragua. Before then, I plan to see firsthand what we're up against."

"May I say something, Colonel?" Honey managed.

"Sure, Major. Go ahead."

"Colonel Solice, we—ah, the hospital requires all of the interpreters. How else can we diagnose?"

Jay formed an expression of regret. "Major, you know how it is with the Legion. The troops in the field have first priority. The Legion mission is to kill the enemy. That goes for hospital availability also, as well as demands on the interpreters. When we send wounded back, we expect them treated first, ahead of any and all civilian cases. But I'll strike a bargain with you. How many crack linguists do we have?"

"Five," Honey answered, still riled at the cold facts, though well aware of their purpose. "And I can make do in Spanish."

"Alright then. I'll see to it that you receive the most proficient interpreter to work the hospital, also a couple more Spanish-language types. All the rest go with me."

Turning away, as a sign of dismissal, Jay led his troops into bivouac.

Tauntingly insubstantial, the white oval wavered in and out of focus. It rocked and sloshed like a small boat in heavy seas. Slowly, Margaret Ainsley-Trowbridge fixed her unsteady vision on the porcelain rim of the toilet basin, only inches from her face.

"God!" she croaked. "Oh, God, God, God."

Her eyes burned and itched and wouldn't cease running a burning stream of water. Her leg and belly muscles threat-

ened to cramp. Her crotch felt like a forest fire. Why? Why
had she done it . . . again? These orgies of drinking and
wild, often kinky, sex didn't prove anything. Worse, they
didn't solve anything, didn't make the hurt go away.

"*B-pik*! Urrrup–b-pik!" Margaret began to hiccough and
belch alternately.

Her intestines stirred and she bent forward over the
bowl. With wracking, gagging coughs, she regurgitated
again. Only a thin, yellow-brown bile spewed into the
clouded water. Nothing left but her stomach to follow it,
she thought with icy resignation. Without looking that way,
one hand fumbled for a glass, found it, and brought it close
to rinse her mouth.

Jesus! Vodka. The gag reflex began without conscious
effort and she suffered through long, agonizing seconds of
the dry heaves. Maybe . . . maybe she should have listened
to the old bag. There . . . were . . . other ways . . . to . . . to
mourn. Maybe it wasn't too late? She could try again? Get
a hold on her life? A loud bang and tinkle of glass followed
the door being thrown violently open.

"Hey, bitch. Git back in there and let's fuck."

Oh . . . my . . . God! Big, stoop-shouldered, ugly, a thick
mat of black hair covering his entire body, he stood there,
wavering in drunkenness. His reddened penis had shriveled
to a third its former size and swung slackly in front of his
scrotum. He was a vision of revulsion. A civilian, a horny,
smut-talking, dock-whalloper she had picked up in a
Charleston tavern and smugged back to Cat Cay under a
lap robe on the floor of her car the previous night. He had a
number of original kinks that had for a while taken her
mind off the terrible hurt that festered in her chest. He'd
also been a cruel, stupid brute.

"No!" Margaret shouted, recovering part of herself.
"No-no-no-no."

In a single, smooth, yet pain-filled move, she sprang up
and around him and dashed to the bedroom. She grabbed
up a sheer peignoir and draped it over her shoulders as she
darted through the house and bolted out the front door.
Barefoot, bedraggled and terribly alone, Margaret stood on
the front lawn.

"Help me!" she cried in a little-girl voice. "Someone please help me!"

INVASION!

Headquarters received word of Nicaraguan troops crossing the border into Costa Rica barely in time to make the announcement so that most of the troops could be moved to TV sets for the Noon News. All stops had been pulled for this juicy media event. Not since Vietnam—the Soviets getting the snot kicked out of them by a small, uncoordinated rebel force in Afghanistan had not been deemed "newsworthy"—had the network newswriters been able to unleash their best apocalyptic purple prose and bombastic broadsides. The network reporters, true to form, heaped fulsome praise on Daniel Ortega and the Nicaraguan army for exercising such humanitarian forbearance during the slashing advance into Costa Rica. If they kept it up long enough, some Legion wags suggested, Ortega might be nominated for a Nobel Peace Prize.

"After practicing great restraint, waiting for international sanctions to be brought against Costa Rica for harboring the mutinous International Brigade, a situation which never materialized, President Daniel Ortega of Nicaragua signed an executive order two hours ago, dispatching an expeditionary force into Costa Rica to make contact with and neutralize the outlaw mercenaries," a pleasantly smiling Peter Jennings informed his audience. "Less than an hour ago, that small detachment left its base at an advance military camp on the southern shore of Lake Nicaragua. It is too early to gauge reaction on Capitol Hill to this latest development, though it is certain President Ortega's actions will meet with the approval of Congress. Aerial reconnaissance over the Miravalles plateau has indicated that the mutinous International Brigade is fleeing along the Frio River."

"Sure," Charley Smith crowed. "On the nearest-that-can-be straight line for San José. Any odds against those two outfits joining up to *take* Costa Rica?"

". . .——sistent rumors that Hunter's Liberty Corps, a

powerful military organization remarkably similar to the mutinous International Brigade, has secretly stolen away from their fortress stronghold on Corsair Cay, headed for Costa Rica, with the possible goal of aiding the International Brigade fugitives, has so far not been verified."

"You don't know the half of it, asshole!" Charlie Smith brayed, shaking a stiffly extended middle finger at the screen.

CHAPTER
9

Col. Norman Stand Watie turned from his office television to catch the phone on the first ring. At the far end, the President's voice, it wouldn't be anyone else, sounded metallic over the scrambler.

"Well, they sort of anticipated us there, didn't they?" Dalton Hunter asked calmly. "No matter. The gentlemen from Costa Rica have all suddenly agreed that a somewhat limited war is preferable to being on the wrong side of a conquest. You've got your request for assistance. It's a green light, Norm."

"Just from this announcement?" Watie asked, elated and wanting to get into motion at once.

"Sort of. It seems that the idealist down there finally got it through his thick, fuzzy-brained skull that expecting peace and nonaggression from Danny Ortega was like sleeping with a king cobra and not being bitten. Whatever, it's your ball game now. And good luck . . . General."

"Gen—. . . what's that?"

"General Watie, of course. Congratulations. Give my regards also to Commodore McDade. Admiral O'Fallon is relieved of his training assignment and attached to the Task

Force as naval liaison and advisor for the duration of this campaign. Go kick a little tail, General."

General Norman Stand Watie marveled at how quiet the Merlins operated. With three of the five smooth-running powerplants behind the cockpit, the speedy little craft had less ambient noise than the forward, upper lounge on an old 747, or the new 927s that plied the upper atmosphere. En route to the carrier, which had been renamed *Scipio Africanus*, aboard a Merlin 2000-I, Watie reflected on the turn of events. The promotions were great news. Although Admiral Thomas O'Fallon howled like a banshee at the renaming of the carrier, and had sulked a full day over his reassignment as naval liaison, everyone else greeted the changes with pleasure. Yet, look where that left Stan McDade. He'd have the best of all possible situations on this operation. All Stan would have to do would be to live in luxury aboard a floating palace and move pins around a map in the war room. Uh, correct that to—what is it?— the, ah, Combat Information Center.

Gen. Watie chuckled at the image and reminded himself of the awesome responsibility in lives and equipment McDade would have, and the simple fact that a single, unforeseen event, or an advance in Soviet technology, even a glitch in one of the defense systems, might put the *Scipio* on the bottom, with its tiny support fleet beside it. No, he didn't envy Stan at all. A streamlined, deltoid shape flashed past, then fell in line to escort them to the carrier deck. In the end, Watie concluded what really mattered was that it was happening again and he was right there to command the Legion.

All due ceremony attended Gen. Watie's arrival on the *Scipio*, and the Legion Commandant detected a glint of smug satisfaction in the eye of Admiral Thomas O'Fallon. Everything had gone smoothly, even the boatswain's call of, "The *Legion* is aboard," referring to Watie's position, had been letter perfect. After the formalities had concluded, a Legion Captain, now an aid to *Commodore* McDade, stepped forward.

"Let me escort you to the CIC, General," he offered.

Inside the huge island of the carrier, noise diminished dramatically. The metal walls didn't even reflect their footsteps on the tough rubberoid material lining the deck plates. The aide in the lead, they descended two levels and entered a large, semidarkened room. Huge plastic, vertical, see-through serial display maps represented their immediate surroundings and important quadrants around. There being no tactical operations ongoing, these were not manned. A gigantic map table dominated the center of the room.

A new addition, it was done in three dimensions with the contours of mountains, valleys, and waterways represented in proper colors. An aerial grid was suspended above, on four short legs and a central cable that extended to the ceiling. *Overhead*, Watie reminded himself, trying to dredge up all the proper naval terms. The area depicted was Central America. Commodore McDade began his briefing without preamble.

"The Nicaraguan forces are arrayed here, here, and here. Our information is being constantly updated by Air Force AWACs and satellite photos. The concentration of Sandinista armor at San Carlos was a feint, and those units are now moving by barge across the lake, to disembark on the Pan American Highway."

"Excuse me, Col., er, Commodore," a young, female Legion officer interrupted. "Daniel Ortega is on Radio Sandino. Would you care to have it piped in?"

"Of course," McDade responded.

Voice-over English translation masked the dictator's words. "It is our desire to assure the peace-loving peoples of this hemisphere, and their governments and the governments of the world, that Nicaragua is not acting in the role of an aggressor. Our sole purpose for entering Costa Rica is to reduce the threat to our frontier. Nicaraguan troops are moving via the Pan American Highway in an attempt to cut off the mutineers, who are struggling through the lowlands with Sandinista infantry in pursuit. We do not wish to acquire territory, nor will we violate Costa Rican airspace . . . unless provoked."

"Christ," Watie grumbled, "we'll play hell blocking anything if we can't use the Merlins."

"I'd use them in a hot tick," Stan McDade responded. "Ortega's trying to turn this into a race without opposition clear to San José. We won't overhaul the *General Patch* and the *Meteor* until twenty-two hundred and they can't even dock at Puerto Limon until a little after oh-four-hundred tomorrow. Even if the trains are there as promised, the Sandinistas will have captured Puntarenas by the time we're rolling." Stan shook his head.

"We have only one Cohort, reinforced by all of our armor and artillery support equipment. Worse, we'll never get it into action in time."

"That miserable son-of-a-bitch is going to make me out the aggressor," Watie lamented.

"Oh, bullshit," McDade countered. "He's already launched an invasion. Who is stupid enough to listen to him?"

"Just hide and watch," Watie gloomed. "Can we operate closer inshore? And are your aircrews up to night operations?"

Stan looked thoughtful. "Yes to both. Provided we don't have to recover aircraft before dawn. That should optimize range."

"You won't be recovering any of your Merlins. I want them to land at San José," Watie informed Stan.

Considering it, Stan spoke his impressions aloud. "They'll burn anything but bunker fuel in a pinch, and I can ferry ammo and ground crew to them by chopper. Reinforcements and heavy equipment will have to come on a turnaround by the transport ships."

"We can't wait for the *Patch* and *Meteor* to make another round-trip to bring in the other four Cohorts," Watie declared. "I'll have to see if Hunter can shake loose some Air Force transport. We need warm bodies and we need them now."

Intent upon establishing his presence in northern Nicaragua, Lt. Col. Jay Solice targeted the river village of Bocay, where his guides insisted a small Sandinista garrison existed. Jay had observed that "his" Miskitos carried cheap portable radios and recalled that a Miskito-language radio station broadcasted from Puerto Lempira, Honduras.

"It's called Radio Sani," Jay informed his S-2. "The name means grapevine in Miskito. Appropriate enough, considering that in addition to gossip, music, and news, encoded messages are transmitted to YATAMA operatives. There's not a lot floating around about this outfit. I ended up searching back issues of *Soldier of Fortune* and *Eagle* magazines for references to the area. Struck gold in the January eighty-eight issue of *SOF*. God, that seems like a century ago. Given the time allowance, both since the article was written and what we had before departure, I didn't locate the author, Wayne Sumstine, for a personal briefing, yet the article itself proved invaluable. Given ten years to perfect their act, I imagine it's doing rather well now."

"Couldn't we have gotten better information from the Pentagon, or the CIA?" the youthful captain inquired.

Jay gave him a wry look. "I suppose we could have, provided they'd been in a mood to cooperate. You know how at certain times during each day, our Indians have ears glued to the speakers of their pocket Jap jobs? I'm guessing that's when Radio Sani sends its coded instructions. You'll also note no one has bothered to inform us of the fact. I want you to get your hands on a pocket radio and tune in that frequency when you see our guides listening carefully. Don't be sneaky about it. Let 'em see you and we'll check the reaction you get."

That analysis prevented any great surprise late the next afternoon when Jay's column was met by a YATAMA patrol. Through one of the guides, they conveyed the information that the team was to follow them. Led into Bocay village, Jay and his men found a meeting set and ready for them. Surprise did assail him, though, when introduced to YATAMA leaders Wycliffe Diego, Brooklyn Rivera, and Steadman Fagoth. The hard-bitten, professional rebels came right to the point.

"We want an honest evaluation of Legion intent, and probable repercussions to our organization," Wycliffe Diego stated flatly.

Briefly, and succinctly, Jay spelled it out for them. He put particular stress on the point that the Legion would train men to fight for their country or be able to take it back. Likewise that when the commitments had been filled by the Costa Rican government, the Legion would positively withdraw. The men of YATAMA were amazed at such candor. Their experiences with government and with soldiers had not been nearly so favorable. Brooklyn Rivera spoke next.

"Some of our, ah, field recruiters tell us that you are, ah, an *indio*. Is this so?" Sly amusement lighted his eyes.

Jay flashed a broad, white smile. "That's right. I'm an Apache. Our Legion Commandant is a Cherokee. In a way, I find it ironic that an Apache is sent into this jungle to negotiate a treaty with an Indian tribe, on behalf of the President of the United States." At their blank looks, Jay went on to explain about Indians and treaties with the U. S government. Then talk turned to the purpose of their meeting.

"We have reached accommodations of sorts with the Sandinistas," Wycliffe Diego pointed out. "They maintain garrisons in the larger communities, from the largely Negro town of Bluefields, north to Cabo Gracias a Dios. At one time they sought to drive us all out, to kill everyone and give our land to favorites of the Party. That is no more. The Miskitos don't bother the Sandinistas so long as they confine their activities to the small *'español' barrios* and don't interfere with Indian or Negro institutions."

Steadman Fagoth snorted derisively. "Most anyone can tell you that this situation will continue only until the communists feel they are strong enough to crush Miskito resistance. When the Contras fought them here, and in the south, out of Costa Rica, they had too much to contend with. That's all over now. Many of our people believe we will not last out a year. With help from your, ah, Legion, that might not be so."

"You speak with an open heart," Brooklyn Rivera began before Jay could react. "This is a good thing. You are a soldier, a warrior like ourselves, *como no*? It was our intention to tell you 'thank you for the equipment, now leave,' thinking you to be yet another politician with empty words and a secret heart. You say you are independent of the American politicians, who are worse than the Sandinistas because they claim to be one thing and yet are another. If that's so, we would now ask you to help us in our fight."

"It is true we need aid," Wycliffe Diego joined in. "We must have weapons and ammunition, medical supplies, and men to teach us the tricks of our enemy."

Jay had not expected such an outpouring. It set him aback a moment before he could rally his thoughts. "There is a very small chance that the Legion may be able to continue aid to your people after we pull out. The best possible conditions would see the Legion sparking a counterrevolution that will crush the Sandinista regime entirely, before world opinion turns against us."

It seemed so remote a scenario that Jay couldn't bring himself to mention it before. They received it without comment, though their eyes glowed with the visions such an offer created. Jay decided the time had come to drop the other shoe.

"Of course, such a risky undertaking would require some sort of payment on your part. All we ask is that you help us in the initial stages of our operation against the Sandinistas."

Two frowns out of three faces. Wycliffe Diego spoke at last. "This is something we must consider. Will you leave us, please, until we make our decision?"

"Certainly," Jay responded, trying to make it light to mask the stress that boiled his stomach into a cauldron of acid. He knew for certain he could not succeed without their active support. The whole Legion diversion, their *maskarovka* as the Russians would say, depended upon YATAMA participation.

An hour of insect-harassing jitters passed before a youthful YATAMA fighter came to Jay's temporary camp and summoned him. He entered the small room of the dirt-floored building to find the three leaders looking much as before. Jay could read no hint of the verdict from their expressionless faces.

"We have decided to give you what help we can," Wycliffe Diego announced into a pregnant silence. "Which is to say, *all* the help we can."

Jay wanted to do a victory dance. He grinned broadly and shook hands around. "Congratulations, gentlemen, on not buying a temporary peace, but instead a sure course to freedom."

"We considered long and hard," Steadman Fagoth informed him. "With your Legion to help us, we see this way as the only hope of our people's survival."

"Now that is taken care of," Brooklyn Rivera injected, along with the first smile from the trio, "when do we start this little war of yours?"

CHAPTER
10

One hundred fifty miles to the target. Then seventy-five back to San José. Captain Arizona Jim Levin studied the computerized scroll map of their mission while he led a long string of tiny Merlin 400s over the small bay of Bahía de Moin and the city of Limón, Costa Rica. Below, the *Meteor* and the *Alexander H. Patch* discharged their respective cargoes onto the floodlighted banana docks. Long lines of Legionnaires shuffled along the rough, irregular planks of the former United Fruit Company facility to the trucks that awaited them.

The ships had responded to Watie's call for more speed and arrived at 0300 hours. Jim's flight of Merlins had been launched before unloading had begun. Now the anthill scene dwindled behind him as Arizona Jim punched in the flight director and autopilot of the Merlin for the first leg of their journey. Flying at three thousand feet and throttled back to three hundred mph, the little birds' low noise signature blended with the ambient sound level of the city so well that no one suspected their presence. No more had they detected the swarm of 2000 models that had preceded them. The civilized coastal strip, looking like a scattering of sparks, soon disappeared behind him.

Hands shaking with precombat jitters, Jim eased down

to nap-of-the-earth, when all too soon the Satellite Nav System bleeped a warning. From here on he'd fly it on his own. Outside the cockpit, ghostly green in his LCNVGs, the forested hillsides flitted past at an alarming rate. This treetop level approach would ensure no acquisition by enemy radar whatsoever. Suddenly a pale chartreuse ribbon appeared across his line of sight and Jim fed the course correction to the flight computer with a slight movement of the stick in his right hand.

"Arms up, Becky," he muttered.

"Arms up, Jim," the little ship responded in its soft, feminine contralto imitation of Julie London. "Give 'em hell, Tiger."

A grid gently glowed to life in Jim's vision as his *H*ead *U*p *D*isplay came on. It quickly confirmed the ready condition of the ship's fighting systems. "Toltec flight, this is Toltec zero-zero. Maintain fifteen-second intervals at three-seven-fiver knots and follow me," Jim spoke on his squadron net.

With contact imminent, Jim's involvement in many tasks began to settle his nerves. The mission occupied all of his resources. Abruptly a troop-covered T-72 bloomed in the HUD stadia. Reflexively thumbing his chain gun, Jim watched in sickened amazement as the little 30mm shells triggered off reactive armor and scattered pieces of Sandinista infantry all over the immediate landscape. The winking of yellow light from a second tank's turret top informed Jim that the vehicle commander had visual and a 12.7mm DShK on him. This time Jim correctly fired one of his six three-point-five rockets.

The buffet of its explosion lifted Jim off line for a shot at a BMP. Then a Zil truck bracketed in the stadia and the chain gun strung hot steel into the careening vehicle, firing the fuel tank as troops spilled from the rear. A rocket beeped its readiness for a run to a tank and Jim freed it. The 3.5 missile struck at the rear of the T-72's turret, in the juncture between it and the body. The low, domed dish, its long gun whooping as it spun, sped off through the trees like a giant hockey puck, to shatter trunks and fall saplings. Green Soviet tracers laced the night. Yellow flames made a devil's dance against the high base canopy of jungle. The orgy of destruction continued until Becky's sexy voice called out.

"Take us home, Boss. We're out of ammo."

Only then did Arizona Jim notice the pair of flashing red lights on the instrument panel. For a moment he could not recall the verbal response. He started to reach for a switch, then dredged up the cue he had programmed in.

"Message received, m'dear. You can stop winking at me."

The warning lights blinked out. Jim looked around at the terrible damage his flight still wreaked upon the Sandinista column. "Your place or mine, Big Boy?"

It probably had a lot to do with the after-action euphoria, for he had programmed Becky to do Mae West himself, yet he never had found it quite so hilarious before. Tears ran as he began to nose up and pull away from the carnage.

He still chuckled when he reached the apex of his pull-out and glanced down at the rest of his wing. In the blink of an eye, he saw one of the hundred forty-nine little birds slam into a tank and erupt in a fireball. Sobered, and feeling guilty for his levity while his men remained in danger, Jim retraced the ravaged column. His amazement grew as he tallied the surprising number of tanks still in operation, though hemmed in by wreckage and illuminated by fire. Jim tried not to see the twisted, blackened, sometimes burning stick figures of dead and maimed human beings. Two more vehicles blew up as he keyed his mike, a testimony to the determination and marksmanship of his wing.

"This is Toltec zero-zero. Form up on me. Next stop, Saint Joe."

The last of his warbirds had yet to disengage and join formation when a flight of four Legion Harriers whistled over, on their way to Nicaragua with area denial weapons pods on their bellies. Jim craned his neck to watch them, mindful of the destruction that those powerful cratering bombs and nasty mines would bring.

"Becky, m'dear, I believe those Harriers indicate that the Sandinista airbase is about to be destroyed, ah, yes."

Taking her cue perfectly, the computer answered with a

programmed sexual innuendo that roughly translated as "Does not compute."

Stars broke through the thin, high-altitude overcast during the final leg of the journey. Arizona Jim thrilled to the sight. Nowhere, other than his beloved Arizona desert, had he seen so many stars so bright. The flight remained uneventful. A landing strip and service area had been set up for them at a large park on the edge of San José, Costa Rica, located next to the National Sports Palace, soccer fields and equestrian arena. The landing was as normal, and as boring, as an approach to the pea-patch airport in Douglas, Arizona.

"Kilo Approach, this is Toltec zero-zero. We're on straight in final from area ops. We'd like clearance to land, over."

"Toltec zero-zero, this is Kilo Approach," a monotone voice answered Jim's call. "You're cleared for a straight in. Report the strobe beacon at the threshold. There'll be a Follow Me vehicle on the runway to direct you to where you are to let down. Set altimeter to two-eight-niner, winds ten knots from two-six-five. Welcome to San José."

On the ground, Jim quickly learned that the Merlin 2000s, under command of Don Beisel, had caught the ready squadron of the Sandinista air force on the ground and effectively destroyed it. Only ten aircraft remained, some of them damaged. The four picket aircraft had not been alerted until the first rockets fired and they were soon flamed by the hot little interceptor Merlins at a cost of two birds dead. That was the good news. Jim soon got the bad.

"Sorry, we've not had time to ferry in the ground crews, Captain," a tough, potbellied Aviation Services master sergeant informed him. "The choppers have brought in a respectable supply dump, but no warm bodies. There's every sort of ammo and plenty of fuel for these things. Also some of the new self-annealing patches for those bullet holes. But . . . you'll have to do it yourself. Things will be back to normal tomorrow."

"Yeah," Jim offered laconically. "All fucked up."

* * *

Towering flames and black, oily smoke from burning jet fuel totally eclipsed the rosy glow of impending sunrise in the eastern sky over the airstrip at San Miguelito, Nicaragua. Soviet advisor, Leiutenant General Boris Nikitavich Sobolin, harangued his Sandinista counterpart as that worthy frantically directed firefighting and damage assessment crews.

"You saw it," the beet-faced Russian screamed. "You saw them come screaming in here with all the precision and panache of the bastard Americans' Blue Angels. Yet your defense forces did nothing about it until it was too late."

"We did what we could. The radar was out. We had an earlier attack, as you should recall, Comrade General, and with all the confusion, no one saw those Harriers approaching."

"Not until they belched a great gout of flaming smoke from each side of their belly pods," General Sobolin snarled.

He recalled the earlier raid clearly. Small, speedy, odd-shaped craft seemed to materialize out of nowhere. Neither radar nor infrared could lock on their signal. They had swarmed over the field and obliterated the hangars, aircraft revetments and...and an entire squadron of MiG-25s. Preposterous. Yet it had happened. Two fuel dumps and an ammunition bunker destroyed. Their six patrol planes had managed to down two of the enemy. Only two! Then had come the other attack, as the unnatural aircraft sped away to the southwest.

Tiny, fast-falling black parachutes blossomed as *MUSTA* and *MIFF* submunitions erupted from the shrieking Harriers, and soon stabilized. Then *STABO* runway-cratering charges began to hash up the flight apron. Suddenly, everything before his eyes turned into a bright yellow pattern that seemed to rush outward from his chest, only to be sucked back as darkness and more confusion.

Lt. Gen. Sobolin had been knocked silly by too close a proximity to a detonating *STABO* bomb. He did not see his Nicaraguan counterpart leap up, unmindful of the automatic cannon fire and bursting ordinance, and begin to di-

rect a crew to start clearing smashed concrete from one of
the smoking holes. Nor did he see the little *MUSA* mine
when it leaped into the air and burst with a terrific concus-
sion that cut down the salvage team with hundreds of tiny
steel balls. The Sandinista general ran to a nearby bull-
dozer, climbed aboard and directed the operator to clear
away the rubble. When it started off, Gen. Encines darted
off to find a firetruck, any firetruck.

Within twenty feet, the dozer hit a *MIFF* mine and was
transformed into scrap iron. The human driver departed
rapidly for the big commune in Hell. At that point, a sort
of groggy reality reimposed itself on Lt. Gen. Sobolin.

Regaining enough wit to realize what had happened, he
shouted to the terrified Sandinistas not to move. All but
frothing at the mouth, he began to curse.

"It's the Legion. It has to be the fucking American Foreign
Legion. The damned Legion has sewn this area with those
doubled damned bombs from RTG in West Germany."

That's when he saw the Sandinista general standing in
the midst of the flaming rubble, sobbing wretchedly. Immediately he began to verbally lash the Latino officer, up-
braiding him for a plethora of imagined faults, errors, and
omissions. When Sobolin finished his tirade, silenced by
the need to draw another deep breath, the Sandinista general eyed him with the glittering obsidian orbs of a deadly
little green tree snake.

His own emotions under reign once more, his Latin tem-
perament controlled after the horrible disaster, he answered
in a low, icy tone. "Comrade General, go fuck yourself,
you Soviet *gringo cabron*."

Having expended his ground attack weapons and accomplished his mission, Capt. Tom Allbright pulled his Harrier
into a steep climb and spared a glance at his systems display, then thumbed up the anti-air mode. The screen became a display from a madman's video game. Bogeys all
the hell over the place. His threat analyzer screamed at him
that there were more missiles than manned aircraft out
there after him. With no time for regrets, Tom released the
weapons pod from the belly to reduce weight and drag,

then slammed into a hammerhead turn as only a Harrier could do it.

Two AA-8 Aphid missiles, on divergent courses, sizzled through the airspace the Harrier should have been occupying. Tom jerked his nose up, the big Rolls Turbine at maximum thrust in the hover mode, nearly driving himself through the seat as the Harrier skidded to a near stop. Huge and hideous, two MiG-25s howled over, their vortex slapping the jump jet's nose back down as Tom began to rotate from hover to flying on his wings again. At last he managed to bracket one of the fleeing fast movers. Too close! Yet its afterburners roared at full blast and Tom knew he'd have more than enough time to dodge the effects of the Aim-9 Sidewinder, even as he fired it.

What the hell, he considered philosophically, it would give the Sandinistas something to do while Tom took care of another problem. The other problem identified on his threat analyzer as an AA-7 Apex, probably fired from long range, though still closing fast. Too fast. Tom jinked wildly as his ship fired a decoy flare, then rode out the slam when the proximity fuse detonated the missile. He winced as he listened to the *ping* and *thock* music of fragments striking his craft.

Unbelievably he was still flying. Tom looked around and found his entire flight similarly engaged. Slowly a savage grin split his thin lips. Too good at maneuvering to be Latino pilots, these Soviets had a great deal to learn about Harriers. The first lesson he intended to teach was that the great speed of a MiG-25 could be a handicap. The second lesson was that no missile system in the world could maintain a lock-on if the Harrier pilot saw it in time.

"*Dosvedahnya vee Ruski obelyoodaki*," Tom purred as he maneuvered to suck in one of the unwary. "Adios, you Russian bastards," he repeated in English.

While he politely acknowledged introductions to the latest raggedy-assed band of YATAMA fighters, Lt. Col. Jay Solice mentally kicked himself for not bringing in any of the Legion's 7.62x39 ammo from the Honduran base camp. Inquiry confirmed his self-castigation when the five men proved to be armed with three worn-out AKs and two single-shot shotguns. They were able to produce sixteen rounds between them; three 12 gauge with 6 shot, and thirteen rounds of 7.62 Soviet. His chagrin evaporated when Jay considered that these men, and others like them, had held at bay the most heavily armed fighting force Central America had ever known for more than ten years.

Yep, Chesty Puller had read his history alright, Jay reflected. He was aware that the ancestors of these fighting men had been hired as mercenaries by the Conquistadores. Chesty had made good use of this by recruiting them into Company M. Thereby, Chesty justly built for himself a reputation as one of the rootin'-tootin'est Marines in an outfit with a whole galaxy of heroes. Jay liked that turn of phrase. Recalling the famous George Patton line, "Rommel, you magnificent bastard, I read your book," Jay chuckled, suddenly feeling better about the whole campaign.

Old Truman Cunningham, the most fluent of the interpreters, came to him. "*Coronél*, we are approaching the gold mining town of Bonanza. It has a large '*español*' population and a garrison of Sandinistas. We soon be ready to attack."

"What about patrols?" Jay inquired. "Or prospectors wandering the hills?"

"No danger from the soldiers. They stay close to the *cantinas* and the women of Bonanza. The Sandinistas say the gold belongs to the state, so no more prospectors. Even if so," Cunningham went on, "they not report us."

Lt. Col. Solice considered this for a moment. The long trek into the mountains had been hard on his barely acclimated troops. And a dawn attack always had a certain appeal.

"Alright, tell the troops to shuck their packs. We'll spend the night here and move into position for an attack at first light."

It didn't take a great deal of genius to recognize the subtle change in the Miskito attitude. Lt. Cato Padilla saw it everywhere in the base camp. Children no longer went

about with grubby faces, eyes haunted, and bellies swollen
from hunger. The women chattered and worked willingly
to further improve the remarkable new housing they en-
joyed. The men took to their training with a will and spirit
that surpassed anything he had previously experienced. Lt.
Padilla's inquiry into the reasons, given his limited ability
in the Miskito dialect, had resulted in scant enlightenment.
Such cheerfulness on the part of refugees in a not-too-hos-
pitable foreign country seemed out of place. As a final
resort, he took to asking one of his interpreters.

"Oh, is simple, *teniente*." The man brightened at the
query. "We are now brothers with the Le-gion. You—how
you say?—stand between us and the Honduras government. You give us food, medicine, a good place to live,
guns. We work for you, do what you say. We do it gladly."

"But your previous ah—ah, reserve?" Padilla stammered.

"That simple, too. Before we be merely polite to
strangers, and maybe embarrassed at receiving gifts from
men who we soon throw out . . . Now Le-gion here to teach
us how better to kill Sandinista peegs. Coronel Jay, him not
lie, not say Le-gion stay, but say we have chance to win.
We fight with Le-gion, kill many Sandinistas, go back to
our homes. This make us happy. Aren't you happy, too,
teniente?"

Was he? Or had it all been better before the Legion came
here?

CHAPTER
11

Nestled at the headwaters of the Rio Bambana, in a southeastern fold of the Cordillera Isabela, Bonanza, Nicaragua, was largely a collection of hovels. Being a mining town, it consisted primarily of saloon hovels and whorehouse hovels, with some grocery, mining equipment, and living hovels scattered along the twisting, dirt, up-and-down streets. The most impressive structures were a flying-buttressed, Spanish colonial style Catholic church, now re-dedicated to the *new* Savior, Che Guevara, by the supposedly neutral bishops of Nicaragua. This had been done at the behest of the communist government of Daniel Ortega, much to the amusement of the Soviet and Cuban advisors.

Other prominent features, left mostly unchanged by the Sandinistas, were the headworks of the mineshafts, and the sandbagged, rockwork fort first installed during the revolution by the forces opposed to President Somoza. It was at the latter place that the haunting notes of a bugle shivered through the crisp air of sunrise, while the red-and-black, horizontal-barred flag of the "new" Nicaragua began to ascend a flagpole that had long since yielded its perfect erection to the prevailing winds.

"*A-ten-cion! Regalos ... armas!*" the fat First Sergeant of the Sandinista garrison commanded.

With the flag secured at the top of the staff, the dull routine of reveille and roll call began. Only to be galvanized into frantic confusion by the flutter of incoming 81mm mortar bombs. While the first deadly roses bloomed on the parade ground, sentries collapsed to unheard fire from suppressed submachine guns. Shrapnel sliced through a surplus of vulnerable flesh and the screams of the wounded backgrounded a Legion sapper team, which emplaced a forty-pound shaped charge eighteen feet in front of the main gate. A scant hundred yards away, shaken by the impacting mortars, a mine superintendent tied the steam whistle open and its strident shriek lent a soprano note of hysteria to the general cacophony.

Listening to the shrill blast from the direction of the mine, Lt. Col. Solice nodded his head as though he had reached a critical decision. From one of the numerous gadget boxes hauled painfully over the mountains he took a large ghetto blaster and checked that it was in readiness. With the volume cranked up to headache level, he pressed the play button and the continuous loop tape cassette began to turn.

A trio of bugles replied to the frantic one announcing the attack. Crystal notes shivered in the cool air, backed by the martial roll of drums, as the first twelve bars of the Legion March sounded ominously across the narrow valley. Leaving the recorder behind, Lt. Col. Solice hurried to join his deploying troops. *El Deguello*, the Cutthroat Song, an appropriate bit of psy-war, Jay thought pleasantly. Ahead of him, he saw a slight puff of white smoke as the fuse igniter sputtered to life in the shaped charge.

Intensely white-yellow, a spot of light developed where the explosive had been. Tinged with red-brown dust, it expanded to strike the main entrance. As though slammed by a fiery fist, the portals burst inward. Like floodgates, the shattered barriers released a torrent of screaming Legionnaires and YATAMA guerrillas.

"*Madre de dios*!" Capt. Julio Guzman, commander of the Bonanza garrison, shouted aloud. "Who are they? Who can be attacking us?"

Too busy dodging mortar fragments, his First Sergeant didn't bother to answer. Men ran helter-skelter across the parade ground. The 81mm projectiles continued to fall. A rain of terror, Capt. Guzman thought absurdly, laughing inwardly at the poor pun. He had to get ahold of himself. He looked to the corner guard towers. Machine-guns should have opened up by now.

At both places he saw the draped bodies of his dead sentries. Only hands cold with death held the Soviet 12.7mm MGs. Capt. Guzman reached out to yank on one, then two more running figures. "You three, up in that tower. Replace the gun crew," he commanded.

Then the front gates blew in, propelled by a plastic explosive wind.

Over the frenzy of a charge with fixed glaudii, Jay gradually became aware that the Sandinista troops were trying to surrender. Unfortunately, the maddened YATAMA fighters ignored this gesture and killed them anyway. A number of Nicaraguan soldiers had rallied around an officer and, as Jay watched, they disappeared into a thick-walled building and began to barricade themselves. From above and behind the Legion G-2, a Russian DShK machine-gun opened up.

"Get a blooper on that," Jay shouted, ducking low and jinking to one side for cover behind a low wall.

A M-203 coughed in a flat note and sent a 40mm grenade on its way. Short by two feet, it detonated against the plastered-over adobe wall. A shower of steel fragments, bits of crimped wire, slashed into a group of surrendering Nicaraguan soldiers below, killing two and a YATAMA guerrilla, wounding five others and two Legionnaires. A second grenade sped from the blooper, to smack into the support stancheon of the machine-gun. Its lethal cargo of wire bits shredded the crew and left behind a scarlet haze. Screams of sheer terror came from a band of unarmed Sandinistas, fleeing vengeance-minded YATAMA warriors.

Two short, stocky Indians caught up with the slower soldiers and yanked them to one side. Deft strokes with machetes severed their belts and slashed open their

trousers, exposing their genitals. When the Sandinistas realized what was about to happen to them, they began to
wail like the tormented inmates of Bedlam. One machete
rose and flicked downward before Lt. Col. Solice could
react.

"That is for my wife, you son of a pig and a whore. This
is for my daughter. She was only seven years old," the
YATAMA guerrilla shouted.

First the soldier's testicles, then his penis lay in the dirt,
useless lumps of flesh now they had been severed from his
body. Shock plunged him into unconsciousness and he bled
to death on the ground. Next to him, his comrade howled
for mercy.

"A little bit at a time," the other YATAMA said pleasantly as he removed two Sandinista fingers with his blade.
"Just like your comrades did to my son. Then we're all
going to use you in the anus like your friends did him. Ten
years old when he learned about Sandinista justice. Afterward, he begged me to kill him, to take away his shame
and the awful pain."

"*Mierda en la lache de tu madre*!" the tortured Sandinista rallied his courage to shout defiantly.

"And I piss in the *mouth* of your mother," came the
implacable reply, while the YATAMA guerrilla deftly
sliced off the Sandinista's nose with another swipe of his
machete.

"Stop it! Stop what you're doing!" Jay Solice roared
through Truman Cunningham's translation.

"They burn our homes, destroy our crops, rape our
wives and children, murder us in our beds. It is not *enough*
what we do to these Sandinistas," one man flung an an-
guished reply at Jay.

Somehow the muzzle of the Sidewinder in Jay's hands
got maneuvered around to point casually at the angry man's
belly. "It is not the Legion way. They have surrendered.
Protect them or..."

Before he could finish his statement, Truman Cunningham interrupted to say what the others already knew.
"You will die with them."

Goddamnit! He may have blown the whole operation,

Jay stewed as he eyed the enraged faces before him. Suddenly he perceived a subtle change in their expressions. Lips quirked here, a nose wrinkled there. Then they were laughing, as the one who had effected the mutilations spoke.

"Then we do it the Legion way. Hah? What say, fellows? The *Legion* way."

A shot cracked from an upper window of the barricaded headquarters building. Several men scattered and Jay cut off a three-round burst. "Get some gas rounds up there!" he called out. "Gas on the headquarters."

A pair of Indians with their newly acquired M-203s and M-16s managed to bloop the big gas cannisters through a window on the first try. With streaming eyes, Capt. Guzman looked again at the men who had destroyed his command. Those uniforms, the crested helmets. He had been in Panama and knew too well whom he faced. He placed a hand on the forestock of his best marksman's rifle.

"Put it down, Umberto. That's the Legion out there. The American Foreign Legion. They will treat us well if we surrender. If we do not, they'll kill us to the last man. You hear that music? No Quarter. They do not jest when they use it."

Within another ten minutes, the fighting ended. At once Jay issued orders to round up the entire population of Bonanza. He soon learned that the residents consisted almost exclusively of "Spanish" miners and their families and a handful of Eastern Bloc mining engineers. There were also two Hindu merchants from India. The "Spaniards" were disposed to welcome the Legion, and made no effort to hide the terror they felt in the presence of the Miskitos.

They remembered only too well how they had stood aside and silently cheered, or actively participated in the program of planned genocide against these people. Instituted as almost the first program of the Sandinista government, the methodical extermination of these Indians had been a personal pet project of that great humanitarian and lover of peace, Daniel Ortega. As recipients of the former Indian ground, these "Spanish" Nicaraguans had done nothing to prevent the mass murders that had gone on since 1979. Supported by their Marxist, knee-jerk liberal comrades in the United States, they had expressed an opinion only in denying that such a thing had happened. Now they all but groveled in the dirt and licked the boots of the Legionnaires, in their eagerness to curry favor and protection from those whom they saw as their only salvation.

Fawning and bleating their innocence, they likewise lavished hatred on the European engineers. Herded together in the plaza, these sterling citizens' voices turned it into a Tower of Babel. With the flaming zeal of converts, they hotly denounced the dedicated Sandinistas among them, the Cuban schoolteachers, Soviet military advisors, and the Europeans. When an armed Indian walked close by, they cringed.

"You stinking scum make me sick," Lt. Col. Jay Solice rapped out at them in his Mexican-accented Spanish. "You have committed, or permitted, enough horrors to condemn you all to *el paridon*." Shrieks of fright and lamentations rose in their midst as they visualized the all too familiar firing wall and the squad of grim-faced soldiers. "But, we of the Legion are magnanimous. It is in my heart that some of you have not lost your *huevos*, that you feel shame for what you have allowed to be done to you. Those who would see their country freed from the communist yoke of the Sandinistas will be trained and issued arms. You will redeem yourselves of a blood debt with the blood of the *comunistas*."

Work set about to loot the town of everything useful to the Miskitos, and in particular the YATAMA fighting force. After Jay's brief encounter with the "Spanish" occupants of Bonanza, one of the "Spanish" males begged him for a private audience. Uncharacteristically, Jay agreed.

"*Mi general*," the craven creature blurted out in a froth of insincere flattery, "I know of one man your, ah, *soldados* have not yet found. He is a *Norteño*, an American like you. A doctor. He is said to be hiding in the church. In the crypt under the high altar. He waits until you leave so he can hurry off and make a report to his Sandinista comrades. You will reward me for this loyalty, *Señor general?*"

"I'm a Lieutenant Colonel and you already have your reward," Jay told him darkly.

"How is that?"

"You're still alive, aren't you?" Jay growled. The informer gasped. "Get out of here. I'll have your story checked out. If it's accurate, you'll continue to stay alive . . . for a while."

Twenty minutes later, the squad Jay had dispatched to the church returned. They frog-marched a short, thin, willowy young man with a limp wrist and a well-developed sense of high dudgeon.

"You can't do this to me. You can't lay a finger on me. I was accepted for sanctuary by the church. You don't dare touch me, I'm a doctor. I'm an American citizen. I'll complain to Amnesty International, to the Human Rights Commission, to—to the United Nations." He finally ran out of places where he could lodge his complaints. Panting slightly he eyed Jay Solice balefully.

"Fuck off," Jay stated flatly.

"Wha——? Now, see here, you have no right to . . ."

Jay's raised hand silenced him. "You've been spouting your shit, now's time you listen. Right now, right here, in this particular little lump of Nicaragua, there isn't a goddamned thing I *can't* do to you. Now you can cooperate, go along and be a good boy and I'll take you back to our base camp. Otherwise, I'll feed you to the crocodiles or the jaguars."

They had through the next day, Jay figured, before any alarm got out to the Sandinistas. All the same, he would feel better, and the prisoners worse, if they made a few miles down the trail before then. He passed the word that everything portable was to be gathered before noon. The strike force would have a hot meal, the others whatever could be scrounged, and would move out immediately after. Jay had finished his excellent roast port, with rice, beans, and fresh fruit, when a contingent of a half dozen "Spanish" males came to him under guard.

"We represent more than one hundred and fifty men who

wish to join the Contras, *Coronel*," their spokesman declared.

They were all young, in excellent physical condition, most likely miners, Jay considered. Poor bastards, they didn't realize that the resistance group was practically defunct since the treacherous American Congress had cut off their aid money and material. They were also, Jay recalled, the ones who had remained silent while the others whined and sniveled.

"I can do this for you. I'll evacuate you with our troops, if you're willing to form a new unit of Contras, under Legion training. Understand that you'll have this one chance. Let down in your training, or betray the unit, and you'll be terminated."

After a moment's conference, they readily agreed. Jay shook hands with each one of them and turned them over to the noncoms. Within ten minutes, loaded with all the captured arms and ammunition they could carry, along with food, medical supplies from the American traitor's dispensary, and all the money in town, the much swollen column made haste out of the area. The prisoners bore the heaviest loads, including ammo, while the volunteers carried the surplus AKs and other firearms. Although happy enough about the captured munitions, the triumvirate of YATAMA leaders came to Jay with concern on another matter.

"You cannot trust them. These Spaniards are two-faced and despicable. You should never have accepted even one of them."

"The way I see it, boys, we can't move beyond Miskito territory without Nicaraguan troops. How, unless we smash the communist leadership in Managua, can we guarantee the safety of your homes?"

It might have been a joyful occasion. Certainly the excited youngsters considered it so. Shouting and waving, they trudged along the streets, while the silent, solemn-faced adults regarded the column of vehicles and marching men with suspicion, fear, or loathing, depending on their beliefs. Surely, it was the first military parade in San José, Costa Rica, in more than a generation. The American Foreign Legion had come to town. First Cohort, along with most of the support Centuries, made their way through the city to their designated encampment with all the grandeur they could muster. General Norman Stand Watie set his troops to immediate work.

Lt. Col. Chuck Taylor he dispatched to establish the basic Legion infantry school at Cartago, where the Costa Rican government had been routing their flood of volunteers. Initially it would be a short training period. Armor and artillery training would come later. So far, Legion Juliet, with its Merlin 2000s, had managed to maintain a degree of air superiority, while Legion Lima and the Merlin 400s had slowed the Sandinista advance to a crawl, in spite of reactive armor on the MBTs. It would give them, according to the overall mission program, enough time to prepare the Costa Ricans to defend themselves.

Provided, of course, that the Legion got enough equipment and men into the country to prevent a Nicaraguan blitzkrieg that would decide the issue differently. To that end, Gen. Watie admitted to considerable relief when Pops announced that President Hunter was on the scrambler line.

"First off, Norm, I want to apologize for the delay in getting the Air Force to lay on transport for your remaining four Cohorts. The problem lies in guaranteeing secure air space."

"Jesus," Watie swore. "There isn't any secure air space around here."

"I know that, and so does Congress. They're using that as a means of preventing any speedy reinforcement for you. Congress has forbidden the Air Force to send in any armed aircraft, and likewise to allow U.S. planes to enter unsecured air space," Hunter explained. "The media is crucifying the Executive Branch in particular," he added ruefully. "They've raised the ancient specter of Vietnam, and are screaming that the Legion is starting a war that will drag on for decades. According to their version, Ortega is a candidate for sainthood, and the Nicaraguan invasion is merely a small incursion to properly handle a situation that can only get worse by your presence in the area."

"Is that the good news or the bad news?" Watie asked sarcastically.

"Wait until you hear the rest and you decide," the President suggested. "Ortega is threatening to shoot down any attempt to airlift the rest of the Legion into Costa Rica. Since his air force is equipped with MiG-Twenty-fives, which were once the fastest interceptors in the world, the public believes he can do it. Especially with a little expert *deyzinformatsaya* courtesy of our network news services."

"Can you bring the rest of the Legion down to Maracaibo, Venezuela, and stand by until I can move the First into line as a blocking force?"

"I've already tried that. The leftist coalition in power there will not allow it. The best I can do is Puerto Rico. Word of Venezuela's refusal has somehow leaked out," Hunter added as an aside. "The general populace in Mariacaibo and several other cities have started riots." The President chuckled lightly. "They hold the Legion in pretty high esteem, you know."

"What are they doing about that?" Watie snapped, worried about the Legion's first defeat of the Pax Legio program.

"Not a whole lot. I believe that troops are not being used to control the violence because the government fears another refusal to march."

"We may have to go back there and kick a little Red ass," Watie speculated aloud.

"Now, Norm," the President injected quickly. "No need to create problems. You have enough where you are. I'll be working through the night on this. The minute something breaks, I'll let you know. Meanwhile, keep your head down. And *don't give any press interviews*."

"It ain't enough I've got Danny Boy's crack troops to fight. I have the press on my tail. I'd like to send them right up to the front, via our one-five-five gun tubes."

"*Norm!*" The President sounded pained. "Leave the media to me. Just fight your war."

"Now *that's* something I can do. G'afternoon, Mister President."

CHAPTER
12

Like ripples in a pond, first came the momentary hush of the noisy jungle creatures, then the flutter-thop beat of rotor blades. A flock of red-green-and-yellow parrots squawked indignantly, ruffled feathers, and hid themselves in the foliage. Moments later, the airborne intruders approached.

Led by a chopper Lt. Col. Jay Solice recognized as the peerless Soviet Hokum gunship, a pair of Mi-8 slicks overflew the jungle some five klicks south of the Rio Coco. Sight of the awesome shark of the air surprised Jay. He didn't think the Russians would let them out of their own country. At the first sound of the helicopters, the harried column hid in the verdant undergrowth each side of the narrow trail they followed. Slowly the rotor-craft quartered sections of the jungle.

If the observers spotted anything the least unusual, the unarmed Hips would lower and disgorge their cargo of infantry. Jay had to admire the way his largely untrained charges maintained control. None of them panicked and revealed their presence in the jungle. Only once, when the searchers drew close, had it been necessary to forcibly restrain anyone.

Dr. Howard Barry, the American volunteer physician,

made a sudden attempt to run out into a small clearing. The Legionnaire assigned to guard Barry made an instant attitude adjustment with ten inches of cold steel against the Marxist medico's throat. Paralyzed with fear, Dr. Barry remained concealed, while the three Soviet choppers moved off to another quadrant of the search pattern. With agonizing slowness, the trio edged away. When the danger had passed, Jay surveyed his worn-out little task force.

Twice during the exfiltration they had made contact. In both instances, villages had warned them in time to lay an ambush and inflict heavy casualties before the frigging Mi-8s showed up and emplaced a blocking force, while the infernal bastards in an Mi-24 Hind shot up the jungle around them. In spite of this, casualties had been light. They had simply dispersed on divergent headings, until the scattered groups could work their ways to a preselected rendezvous. Still, it had been an exhausting and frustrating journey, one that Jay had every intention of improving.

Their best defense against marauding helicopters, the Javelins, had been rendered nearly useless by the thick top canopy of jungle. Jay almost wished he had stuck around the open country at Bonanza to teach the chopper pilots a little respect. Now, cut off from the river crossing, Jay decided to rest his troops. About time too, he reasoned. For although the Miskito element seemed as fresh as when they had started, the Legionnaires, prisoners, and volunteers were at the end of their endurance. First, though, the ritual had to be complied with.

"Alright, people, we take an hour or so while the bad guys play hide and seek. Let's dig in a defensive perimeter and kick back for a bit. For those who are not Legion, remember, *no smoking*."

Jay no sooner had them in defensive positions than voices could be heard on the trail. The fighting elements of the force dived into their prepared holes, while noncombatants were drawn off a short ways and placed under guard. Lousy noise discipline, Jay considered as the sound grew nearer. At about thirty meters, fleeting movement could be discerned through the trees and vines. Insects hummed and buzzed, gathering for a feast off the unmoving men. Jay chewed savagely on a twig and wished for a half dozen claymores. A lighter green than the jungle growth appeared along the trail and the Legion officer sighted in.

Lt. Col. Solice had white-knuckled the military slack out of his trigger and nearly ticked off a round when he focused more clearly on the target. A woman! He eased off and hastily gave a hand signal to hold fire. The woman, followed by four more, came closer. The approaching people appeared to be carrying large baskets and bundles. Two old men, backs bowed with age and their burdens, came next, then a woman with a swarm of naked children, all ten or under. At a distance of two hundred meters, the strange delegation halted.

"*Hola*," one old man called out. "*¿Estan ustedes Contras?*"

Jay answered him cautiously in Spanish. "There are new Contras with us. If you came to help the Contras, you are our friends. Come forward, two of you."

One of the women, with a large bundle, and the old man who had spoken walked down into the keyhole of the ambush. At close range it was obvious they were Miskitos. The heavy container on the man's back clinked musically in an inviting manner. Truman Cunningham stepped out onto the trail to question them. After a few words, he turned, beaming.

"They are Miskitos, from the village of Sih. They bring food and drink for the fighting men. The old man says they hate the Sandinistas. Their young men have been shot in the fields by the army, their young girls violated by the soldiers, and their crops confiscated for the good of the State, though he doesn't know exactly what that means."

"Have them come forward, two at a time," Jay declared.

In no time, the encounter took on a picnic atmosphere. The women's bundles contained tamales, roasted goat, and slabs of pork—which they chopped fine and blended with fresh coriander, chili pods, and coarse salt—stacks of tortillas, fried plantains, and fresh fruit. The men had containers of cool soda and beer. A royal feast after the cold C Rations and body-temperature LURPS the column had been consuming for several days. One observation kept Lt. Col. Solice on edge.

Fortunately the Sandinistas followed the Soviet doctrine of having troops from one area operate in another. Had the terrain not been strange to them, Jay considered, might the strike force have come as directly and easily to them as these villagers? The opportunity to relax, despite the intensive search being conducted, beckoned to Jay and he decided to stay the night in the present location. They'd cross the river shortly after dawn.

Try as she might, Margaret Ainsley-Trowbridge could not give honest answers to the questions Dr. Cheney asked her. Tall and lean, a well-groomed Vandyke framing thin lips, drawn into a "Vee" smile, Dr. David Cheney, the Legion psychiatrist, sat across his empty top desk from her and steepled his long, artistic fingers.

"That you came here at all, Margaret," he pressed upon her, "indicates that a part of you wants change. Whatever the answers to the questions I asked you, it won't affect our relationship. I'm your doctor, not your judge or jury. I'm not here to determine right or wrong, good or evil. This sort of, ah, exchange is a two-way proposition. What I know of you from your medical records and the tests you took only goes so far. You are young, in relatively good health, you have a good mind, had a promising career, and were happily married. Your husband's death was a traumatic experience. We can't wish it away, but we can find paths around it that lead to a bearable future. But it takes your cooperation to achieve that. So, I'll ask you again, what is it that you 'can't stand to do anymore'?"

Margaret stared blankly at a landscape painting behind the doctor's head and swallowed hard. "I . . . I've been, ah, cheating on my husband," she forced out.

"Your husband is dead. You're a normal woman. Sex is a natural, healthy part of living. An affair or two are understandable."

"That's not it, don't you see? I've been a slut, a whore, a trull. I've . . . I've . . . *Oh, God,* I've been . . ."

Margaret bent double with sobs, her stomach threatening

to rebel and spew out the bitter bile that had accumulated while she waited for this critical interview. Dr. Cheney roused himself from his large, leather-upholstered swivel chair and came around the desk. He knelt at Margaret's side and placed an arm around her shoulders. Gently he patted her like a frightened child.

"Now, now, it'll be alright, Margaret. Let go, let it all out. I'm here to help you."

Some of the potent liquor from Bonanza had been smuggled along, Lt. Col. Solice discovered when awakened from a light doze shortly after sundown. Angry voices rose in growing number as he made his way to the center of the disturbance.

"What's this all about?" he demanded when he came upon five angry Miskitos, one of them holding the arm of a young, attractive Indian girl, and seven of the "Spanish" volunteers.

The Miskitos fingered their machetes and muttered among themselves. Across from them, the Mestizo "Spaniards" brushed the buttstocks of handguns and their personal knives. Through Truman Cunningham, the Miskito spokesman, Brian Cordobes, explained.

"Like always, these Spanish assholes want to take our women. They take this girl. She has not yet seen fourteen years, yet I find one of them rutting with her. He all but had it stuck in her when I laid the edge of my machete against the back of his neck." Cordobes broke into a sardonic chuckle. "He went limp quickly enough then. These other come and grab me, then more of my people come. We . . ."

The girl stood with a thin, cotton dress held in front of her naked body. Eyes wide, a bit unfocused by the aroused passion that had not completely dissipated, she swayed and exchanged glances with her protectors and the men who would have pleasured her. Jay took it all in, remembering that marriages of girls ten and eleven were not uncommon among these Indian and that boys and girls were usually sexually active by seven or so. That had little to do with maintaining order. The Miskitos and "white" Spaniards appeared thoroughly drunk.

"Sergeant Bargas, I want a guard posted over these drunks for the rest of the night. Anyone gets out of line, club him down. Truman, tell Señor Cordobes that the child will not be harmed. Also suggest that he tell her to confine her amorous attentions to her own people. A horny little girl with a pack of males baying at her heels is not a part of this escape and evasion scenario."

"Uh, I don't know how to translate that last part," Cunningham came back.

"Never mind. Just make it clear I hold her as much at fault as the men. Now, I've got to get together with the YATAMA leaders and convince them these new recruits are trustworthy enough to join our fighting force."

Up and moving before dawn, many of the "Spaniards" suffering mightily from hangovers, the Legion column neared the Rio Coco as dawn shed pastel colors on the eastern horizon. Suddenly the point man dropped from sight, his upraised rifle giving the signal of "enemy in sight." The rattle of AK fire followed at once.

"Spread out, spread out," Sgt. Bargas shouted. "Legion to the front."

At first nothing showed but the yellow-orange flickers of muzzle blast. Then the experienced among the group recognized the familiar thunk and fluttering whirr of incoming mortar rounds. Satan's flowers, the mortar bombs began to open ugly blossoms on the river surface, along the edge of the bank and a few yards into the jungle. Like the slithering of giant snakes, shrapnel slashed through the dense canopy, shredded leaves to send them raining down on the heads of the crouching fugitives. Return fire erupted a moment later.

"I'd say they have a good company over there," Lt. Perez estimated to Lt. Col. Solice.

"More like two *poor* companies," Jay returned, humorously emphasizing the quality as well as the number of their enemy.

A sharp battle swiftly developed. The mortar crews

made little improvement on their accuracy. The Legionnaires gave the Sandinistas few targets, and then ones
deadly to them. Some twenty minutes passed when Jay
noted the muted sound of rotor blades. The Puerto Cabezas
based helos moved in, the wicked Hokum in the lead. Jay
watched him come and hoped for an opportunity.

"Get that Javelin ready," Jay snapped a moment later.

This time, anxious for a kill, the Hokum pilot elected to
make a run over the river, passing the besieged fugitives at
an oblique angle that allowed employment of his massive
stores. He could neither see the little light, nor hear the
peep that signaled the Javelin lock-on. The contrail smoked
out behind the Mach 5 missile too late for him to take
effective evasive action.

A bright orange ball occupied the space where the
Hokum had been. Two free-falling rotor blades, all that
remained unshattered from the eight counterrotating main
rotors, fluttered through the air, while the insectile waist
and aircraft-like vertical stabilizer of the murderous bird
upended and plunged into the Rio Coco. The awful blast
punished unprotected ears for half a klick around. With the
air threat so instantly gone, the Sandinistas fired a final
ragged volley and hastily departed. The two unarmed Hips
fled through the air above them. Wisely, Lt. Col. Solice
ordered a half hour wait before authorizing a river crossing.

Natives from the village of Sih produced *doris*, the native dugout canoes, and began the passage with smiling,
laughing faces. They had been inordinately impressed by
the destruction of the Hokum. Likewise had Steadman Fagoth, Brooklyn Rivera, and Wycliffe Diego. The YA-
TAMA leaders met with Jay while the crossing continued.

"We have agreed to fight with your Legion, to be guides
and use your training to teach our young men," Diego
began. "The Rio Coco is my area of operation for YA-
TAMA. What you have done is impressive. Yet there are
too many Spaniards here and I do not trust them."

"You saw how they joined in the fight?" Jay countered.

"Yes. And my friends here are impressed by that. We are
also impressed by the way you destroyed the helicopter.

Still, we believe that we should be allowed to continue the fight against the Sandinistas in our own way. Our men should be led by our leaders. To be commanded by the Legion is to give in to foreigners, like the Sandinistas wanted us to do."

"It's only temporary," Jay urged. "If you think killing that Hokum was something, wait and see what else we can do. Your men will be able to do it, too, if you accept Legion leadership on the broad scope. Individual units will still be led by your own officers. I've also got a way we might get rid of the Hokums until this is all over. I intend to have our commander, General Watie, offer a million-dollar reward to the first Nicaraguan pilot to land one of those Hokums behind Legion lines. I'm not sure this will get us a Hokum to study, it's quite likely it will get them pulled out of action for several months. That's the way it worked when SOF did the same thing for a Mi-24 Hind."

"Who is SOF?" Brooklyn Rivera inquired.

Yep, he was definitely working with primitives, Jay acknowledged. "Some of the people who brought you supplies and supported the Contras," he explained incompletely. "At least do this. Wait until we return. Watch how these, ah, Spaniards behave and work with all of us. Under Legion command this is possible. Without it you are separate factions with a common enemy. Unity of force will bring us victory."

Jay quoted from Von Clausewitz, but to the YATAMAs he might as well have been reading from the *Khama Sutra* in the original Sanskrit. At least they had seen what the Legion could do and he had given the Legion position. All he could do now was wait and see.

CHAPTER
13

Thick smoke, dense flames, and huge clouds of masonry and concrete dust obscured Puntarenas, Costa Rica, from every angle. The staccato crackle of automatic weapons fire had lessened to the point that the pitiful cries of victimized women and the shrieks of tortured children could be clearly heard for more than a klick outside town. Here and there brief firefights broke out, to end all too soon. Hunting rifles and shotguns against AK assault rifles and heavy machine-guns produced devastatingly one-sided results. Angered at delays and frustrated by being cut off five klicks outside Puntarenas, Lt. Col. Asiro Tachikawa sent a team forward with a radio to report on conditions within the city.

"Awh, Christ, it's awful . . . awful," the dispirited voice of the RTO came over the air. His broadcast was being forwarded to Gen. Watie in San José. "The bastards are bu-butchering the children. Women are being raped all over town. Any men that are left are being hunted down and shot."

"What about the International Brigade?" Tachikawa asked.

"Sir, there isn't any fucking International Brigade. There probably never was. The only fighting has been between armed citizens and the goddamned Sandinista army. It's like the Merlin drivers told us. There's no way the air cover could hold on long enough for us to get here. Those Nicaraguan motherfuckers have a whole forest of RPG gunners, and enough twelve-point-seven mike-mikes to bring down anything we put over the city. They're burning, and looting, and raping their way right through the streets. Must be a brigade of troops. Over."

"Any odds our media friends will have footage of this on the network news tonight, claiming it's the work of the International Brigade?" Poet DeVere, Tachikawa's XO, asked cynically.

"I'd say it's about eight to one in favor," the Cohort commander answered seriously. "Pitcher Four-seven, we've heard enough. Pull back to the CP."

"Roger, Baltimore Zero-zero. Out."

"We'll have to reestablish our front beyond that low range," Tachikawa informed his executive officer. "Put everything we have on the line. The passes are narrow and we can dominate the air where their surface-to-air capability is diminished. I'm going to take a little look-see ride before they break out of Puntarenas. We're all that's between the Nicaraguans and San José."

Reacting to a fleeting shadow, the Helio Stallion peeled off and dove for a narrow canyon as a flight of three Su-17s screamed in from the east. Riding shotgun, Lt. Col. Asiro Tachikawa felt his sphincter clutch as smoke puffed from the wings of the lead plane.

"Incoming!" the pilot said into the boom mike as he reached up and triggered a pair of decoy flares. He jinked around a rocky buttress while a pair of AA-2 Atoll missiles streaked from the Soviet fast movers toward the slow, high-winged Stallion. High above the action, two Merlin 2000-Is dropped like stones, fire belching from the hard points outboard the stern fan array. Both AA-2s kept steady on course for heart-stopping seconds. Then the nearest to the target began to verge, following the heat signature of the flare.

Detonated by its proximity fuse, the AA-2 disappeared

in a white-hot ball of debris. Its radar-guided mate surged on, then lost its target in the confusion of reflections and gouged a great gout of earth from the side of the mountain. A moment later, the Su-17s opened fire on the Merlins with NR-30, 30mm gun packs. The three Cuban pilots had to eyeball aim because their instrumentation refused to lock onto the low heat and radar profiles of the deadly, wingless little Merlins.

On the other hand, the Merlins had no such trouble, easily blowing two of the Curaneros into Marxist Limbo. The third went to afterburner and used up his loiter fuel to evacuate the area. Peeking around the side of a mountain, Lt. Col. Tachikawa's pilot saw the flaming wreckage and correctly assumed the coast would be clear to resume the battlefield overview.

"Too bad this is the last day those boys will be around, Colonel," the pilot remarked as the Stallion started a long glide down toward Puntarenas.

"Only too true," Tachikawa agreed. "At least Head-quarters was nice enough to warn me that tomorrow and the next day, the First will be on its own, except for the organic air."

The pilot made a sour face. "The Broncos," he observed, referring to the OV-10Ds, "and these Stallions can't operate without top cover. Not with all we'll be facing."

"I know it. If you can be used to suck their air in close enough, the Javelins will cancel them out, and the Orenda Gatlings will do for incoming missiles. Even then, the risk will be inordinately high. Ah, take a swing along the Pan American Highway. So far their advance has stuck to it. Perhaps we can figure out a few nasty delays for them."

Cohort Sergeant Major Robert Whitaker sat in the rear seat, a steno pad on a metal clipboard, fastened to one leg by a bungee cord. Lt. Col. Tachikawa began to describe the layout of the battlefield along a strip of the highway, leading out of Puntarenas. The portion in question wound between the coast and the foothills of the *Cordillera Tileran* before it swung east, up into the *Cordillera Central* and the San José Basin.

"Make a note that we'll have to take precautions to keep the G-Six guns out of range of the Soviet artillery. I wonder how the bastards will like facing artillery that outranges them for a change? Bridge, ah, five-oh-seven-A," he read off a map. "Mark it for demolitions before nightfall. Between hill six-oh-niner and four-niner-four, a nice little bottleneck. Have Delta Century's British light guns preregister on that. There's another at the canyon formed by the hills nine-seventeen, nine-three-one and ten-two-two on the west and six-niner-niner, seven-eleven and seven-niner-eight on the east. Bridge in square..." Tachikawa went on, describing another for destruction. "Now that bridge over there, Number five-five-zero. It's single lane. Nice bottleneck. We'll mark it for artillery and smart mortar coverage. Okay, now, over this ridge we'll set our secondary line of resistance. We'll force them to fight from the lowlands while we hold the high ground above. That way we can extend our fighting withdrawal over five or more days."

"By then the other Cohorts will be linked up, right?" the pilot inquired.

"If not," Tachikawa told him, "it won't matter. We'll be history."

Bright wake-up sounds came from the refugee portion of the camp on the Honduran hill on the morning after Lt. Col. Jay Solice returned from his recon patrol. Dressed in crisp, clean cammo uniform and new boots, the stocky Apache Legionnaire made a tour of the growing establishment. Lt. Cato Padilla had thrown up a row of six bodegas in his absence, Solice noted. As well as a fairly respectable dispensary and headquarters buildings. Good positions had been picked for the mortars and machine-guns, with solid bunkers for the ammunition. Jay timed his informal inspection so that he ended at the stockade.

"Bring Doctor Barry out, please," he instructed the Legion sergeant in charge.

Sgt. Bobby Raven screwed his face into a mask of disgust. "That one. You're welcome to him, Colonel."

"Good morning, Doctor," Jay greeted the American physician genially.

"It isn't, unless you've come to release me and return me to Nicaragua," Dr. Howard Barry snapped.

"Well, since we're here," Jay drolled, "and it's a long way to anywhere else, I reckon that won't be until the next convoy sets off for San Juan de Flores. I can let you out of there, however. Open up, Sergeant."

"Watch him close, Colonel," Sgt. Raven, a tall, barrel-chested Sioux, cautioned. "He's got the personality of a cobra."

Dr. Barry glowered at the noncom. "You'll all be in front of an international tribunal when I get out of here."

"Don't hold your breath, sucker," Bobby Raven growled.

"*Sergeant*!" Jay said sharply. "We must be courteous to our guests. Come this way, Doctor."

"Where are you taking me?"

"Why, to the dispensary, to put you to work. We have a number of wounded to care for and the usual overload of Miskito patients."

"I'll not be forced to work for you," Howard Barry snapped.

"Oh, everyone works here. It's an old, tried-and-true principle. *Arbeit macht frei*, don't you see?"

Dr. Barry kept his silence on the brief walk to the medical facility. Inside, Jay turned him over to Maj. Honey Simmons. She was all business as she explained the routine to a fellow professional. Dr. Barry glowered at her and affected not to hear a word.

"Well, Doctor," Jay concluded brightly. "You'll probably want to wash up and get some coffee before you start in, so I'll leave you now."

Scarlet flooded Dr. Barry's face. "I'll not treat these damned Indians. They are fugitives from justice in Nicaragua. Criminals. I'll not be a party to aiding them. As for your wounded, they are international hooligans, brigands, and pirates. They can all die, as far as I'm concerned."

Hands on hips, Maj. Honey Simmons examined Dr. Howard Barry as though he was a gobbet of offal cast up from a septic tank. "Excuse me, *Doctor*, but there is your Hippocratic Oath, as I recall," she grated out, fighting her inclination to curse him.

"Such arcane dogma has no relevance in the modern world," Barry stated primly.

"Dr. Barry," Jay began in a tired voice. "The Miskitos have identified you as the physician who assisted the Sandinistas in some interrogations of their people. That being the case, their head men have been after me to turn you over to them for judgment. Since your loyalty is obviously so much greater to Marx's Manifesto than the Hippocratic Oath, that's exactly what I'm going to do."

Face ashen, Dr. Howard Barry began to tremble as Lt. Col. Jay Solice shoved him forcibly from the dispensary.

Wycliffe Diego found Lt. Col. Solice during the noontime break. Jay had just set aside his plate, after a meal of fresh fruit and what he swore was roasted monkey meat rather than chicken as advertised. Diego gestured to encompass the camp and all that Jay had been observing through the morning.

"I am astonished at this harmony," Wycliffe Diego offered as preamble. "Everywhere I look, your Scouts, my Miskitos, and the new, ah, Spanish volunteers are working alongside each other willingly and with good humor. We've discussed it, the others and I. It is decided. With those trained here first, we will reorganize my area of operation along the lines your Legion desires. With the stores and munitions taken at Bonanza, we'll be able to make an effective stand against the Sandinistas. If only we had something to use against their flying weapons."

Taken aback by Diego's cool assumption that the booty from Bonanza accrued to the Miskitos and was now under YATAMA control, Jay found himself hard put to make an answer. Since accepting that position seemed more likely to prevent further dissension, he decided that the Legion could arm the volunteers from the Bonanza with the surplus M-16s brought along for the Miskitos.

"Yes," Jay conceded. "Your men are well outfitted now. As to the enemy air, we have an almost magical craft of our own which might be brought in to take care of the Soviet rotary wing menace. It's called the Merlin."

"You say it is magic?" Diego asked in all seriousness.

"Yes. Even the name. It relates to a legendary magician among the white men." Jay went on to describe the operational characteristics of the Merlin 400. "I plan to request enough of them be sent here to cover our operations for the next several weeks. It will mean transporting a large amount of fuel if your people plan to operate far to the south."

A white smile split Wycliffe Diego's coppery face. "Our coasting canoes can handle fuel, all you need. At least until the Sandinistas get onto what we're doing. After that, who knows?"

Jay made an immediate, and important, decision. He excused himself, entered the headquarters and returned with a large-scale map of Nicaragua. This he spread on the table that had held his lunch. Using a .50 caliber round as a pointer, he began laying out an over-all campaign.

"Here's the road from Puerto Cabezas to Bonanza. Is it the only one?"

"Yes. A few animal trails go roughly the same way. We use them, but the Sandinistas couldn't follow us," Diego informed him.

"Good. Can this single road be held against a breakthrough attempt by the garrison at Puerto Cabezas?" Diego nodded uncertainly. "Given our Eryx and Javelin missiles, the answer is yes," Jay put forward. "But preparations must be made."

"The Sandinistas are now forewarned. A second strike against Bonanza would be much more difficult than the first."

"True enough. Yet the garrison at Puerto Cabezas has a large area of operation. If tactical conditions require them to be spread widely enough, they can't concentrate on Bonanza. First we'll invest every village east to Puerto Cabo Gracias a Dios, Balanca, Kisalaya, Sih, Boon, and the villages at Laguna de Wana and Laguna Dacura. Each detachment will have a shortwave radio, dispensary, and Legion arms. The garrison at Puerto Cabezas will soon be spread too thin to protect any single point. And, given an invasion of Costa Rica, it cannot expect reinforcements."

"Costa Rica has been invaded?"

"Yes, Wycliffe. By Nicaragua . . . and by the Legion. We'll have a large enough force there to demand the attention of the entire Sandinista army before it's over."

"Marvelous! Now, I want to invite you to a great feast to celebrate the new alliance. Oh, yes, even though I don't trust them entirely, there will be representatives of the Spanish volunteers there, too."

"Good morning, beautiful," Capt. Jim Levin said to his computer.

"Thank you, kind sir. You're the most handsome man in the entire Legion Air Force."

"You've got that right," Arizona Jim responded with a marked lack of modesty.

"Oh, pooh. Twelve angels altitude warning, Big Boy. Don't forget we're formation flying today."

Whitecaps sparkled on the azure face of the Caribbean twelve thousand feet below. A little awed at the spectacle, Arizona Jim surveyed the all but horizon-to-horizon spread of widely spaced Merlins. Serving as the eyes, 2000-I models led flights of the comparatively blind A configuration and the Merlin 400s with their lower airspeed. Every bird had been armed with air-to-air missiles, long-range Sparrows to match the radar of the I models, Sidewinders for the attack ships, and Javelins for the little Cavalry birds. Jim's headphones crackled to life when Don Beisel informed the approaching troop carriers that he had them on radar.

"Chickasaw Zero-zero, this is Chickenhawk," came an unfamiliar voice. He pronounced the call sign as "Chicka-saw."

"That's Chicka-shay, turkey," Don Beisel injected by way of acknowledgment.

"Well pardon my tongue, Chickasaw. We have you on visual and are turning over security for the lumbering lunks to you. Do you copy, Chickasaw?"

"That's a roger, Chickenhawk. Have a nice trip home."

"To *Puerto Rico*? Are you kidding, Chickasaw?"

"Negative, Chickenhawk. You could be down there where these people are going. Chickasaw Zero-zero out."

The Air Force pale blue F-111s turned off and headed away in the direction from which they had come. On the Air Flotilla net, Don gave the order to reverse course and the Merlins swooped into 180-degree turns, maintaining flight on the lift bodies to conserve fuel.

"The ball's in our court, Big Boy," Becky observed to Arizona Jim.

"Ah, yes, my dear, that it is."

"I hope you Legion boys know what the hell you're doin'," a new voice opined over the contact frequency, trepidation sounding clearly through the tinny speakers.

"We do, ah, transport leader?" Don Beisel questioned.

"You got him. Long Tom One here."

"Hang in there, ol' buddy. We'll show you the way," Don said lightly.

"Roger, Chickasaw."

Arizona Jim speculated on why the Air Force escort pilot would choose the name Chickenhawk as the flanks of the Merlin line fell back, encircled the transports from over the horizon, and headed once more for the coastline. Another sweep of the azure sky gave Jim a panorama of peace and tranquility. One could even see distant commercial liner contrails, he noted casually. Woops! Those weren't contrails.

"Contact!" the Merlin 2000-I leader shouted a moment later. "Confirm MiG-Twenty-fives at thirty miles, closing and firing. That's Mike-India-Golf-Two-Fivers. Scramble, scramble, scramble."

"Ooooh, shit," Capt. Levin said aloud, then told Becky to up arms in preparation to defend the helpless transports.

Determined to stop a threat before it became one, the Sandinistas threw everything they could muster at the transports. The Merlin 2000-Is were first to discover and engage the MiG-25s, which had fired a long-range barrage before coming into visual contact. They made quick answer with a cloud of Sparrows. Instant confusion began for the Russian-trained pilots.

Unable to get a recognizable signature on radar or IR from the Merlins, the Soviet speedsters in fact were blind to all but the Sparrow missiles which seemed to suddenly materialize on their radar and passive IR screens. Switching to the active mode did little except make *them* better targets. Arizona Jim, along with every Merlin pilot in the sector, released a ball of chaff, which exploded into a small cloud of aluminum foil strips with a flare burning in its center.

AA-6 Acrid missiles from the Soviet-built and -armed birds became confused. Their tiny brains could not distinguish between a real target and the foolers. A dozen of them, then some twenty more, closed to a hundred feet and their proximity fuses detonated close enough to scatter hell out of the chaff, though safely far enough behind and to the side so that the Merlins escaped damage. Impact of Sparrow with MiG was another matter.

Greasy-looking fireballs burgeoned well above the horizon, roiling in yellow, black, and orange. The airwaves were alive with chatter as the pilots verified one kill after another. The second flight of Merlins had engaged and rearranged themselves for another attack wave. A huge, ugly shape, which had so far escaped retaliation suddenly, filled the stadia on Arizona Jim's HUD.

"Contact verified, MiG-Twenty-five, handsome," Beth told him.

"Thanks, I'll kiss you for it later," Jim replied. His thumb touched the fire button and a Javelin sped away.

Impact seemed instantaneous, and a huge fireball slammed down the nose of Jim's Merlin, and burning jet fuel washed over the canopy. For a moment, Jim lost it. With the autopilot disengaged, the Merlin spun toward the waves. Jim's eyes blurred, teared, then began to focus. His returning consciousness registered a strange, whipping sensation in the airframe. *Christ*! Was he stalling out? Full forward on the stick offered a dive.

At once Jim realized his error and he fought to bring the nose up as the odd vibration increased. A blur in front of him suddenly solidified into a large strip of titanium, which had sliced into the vacu-formed Kevlar on his Merlin's nose. It had wedged there, Jim saw, like an out-of-place canard. The wind of the valiant little craft's passage whipped at the obstruction and caused the odd flutter. Work-hardened, the strip abruptly snapped off and cut a long groove in the Lexan canopy. Fearing for his aft array of three ducted fans, Jim swiveled his head and discovered that all three engines were dead. The port side nacelle had nearly sheared off and his remaining Javelin canted at an impossible angle.

"We're in some deep stuff, baby," Arizona Jim spoke unconsciously to his computer.

With the waves drawing closer, he nudged the forward two engines to maximum thrust, then hit the starter for the inboard rear engine. Nothing. Knowing that the little bird would float like a cork if there were no structural damage other than what he had seen, Jim had no fear of a seaborne landing. Supposing, of course, he reminded himself, he could land right side up, without enough power left to hover. Time left to try for that.

Capt. Jim Levin tried the rear starboard engine and nearly sobbed with relief when it caught. He felt the power surge and fought the Merlin into a nose-up attitude. His spirits soared, only to come out as a moan of desperation when he looked back and saw the fuel spray in the wash from the fan.

"Mayday, Mayday. Toltec Zero-zero going in at approximately ten degrees ten minutes north by eighty-two degrees, forty minutes west. Mayday, Mayday. All Legion air, do you copy Mayday?"

With the last of his reserve, using the power of the three functional engines, Jim set the small craft down. A shower of spray washed over the canopy, put a moan to the tone of the fans, then subsided in a series of bounces to the gentle rocking of the waves. Nose slightly awash, Jim cracked the canopy, keyed his emergency radio and sat back. Neck craned to give him a skyward view, he watched the wild air battle and the awkward transports fade off into the west.

"Big Boy, we've got company," the company's sexy voice announced a bit later, revealing none of the icy fear it generated in Arizona Jim's chest.

"What is it?" he inquired.

"Confirm, three Type Twenty-five MiG aircraft. Approaching low, at high speed. Configuration indicates attack run."

Oh, shit. Stranded on the surface, helpless and unable to escape. Death loomed large, a black and grim specter before Jim's eyes. A bright flash of sunlight off silvery metal and he saw them. They howled down on him like ravening Dobermans. The lead element flashed past and began a long, looping turn to perform the coup de grace. Then the Merlin shook and the water quivered in the supersonic wake of an F-111, flying at Mach 2+, which seemed to come out of nowhere.

Missiles ignited from under its wings and sped toward the oncoming bad guys. The first Sparrow struck home, lighting the sky with an incinerated MiG-25. The second went wide of its mark. Two Aim-9 Sidewinders lit off from the F-111. Almost at once the nearer MiG became a Cuban pressure cooker. From Jim's point of view, he couldn't figure how the pilot had achieved lock-on of two separate targets and fired simultaneously, yet the third bird excreted greasy, flame-laced smoke, then detonated with stunning force. Its task accomplished, the F-111 made a final, low, slow pass around the downed Merlin. A grateful Arizona Jim waved once, then ducked inside and lowered the canopy as debris began to fall around him.

"Well, that should hold you for a while," the Air Force pilot's voice crackled on the radio.

"W-who are you, where'd you come from? And, ah, thanks," Arizona Jim babbled in relief.

"It's the Chickenhawk, li'l feller. Chickenhawks attack from high in the sun and eat their prey on the run. I sorta overheard your Mayday accidental like. Since I'm faster than any of your friends, thought I ought to give you a hand. I gotta scoot back to my formation. They'll prob'ly bust me down from Major to First Loo for this, but what the hell? It was fun. And I get to paint three red stars on the side of my ship. You take care, hear?"

CHAPTER
14

First to go had been the birds. Then the small mammals departed. After them went the larger beasts, even the predators and the carrion eaters. Only the insects stayed. In thick clouds they gorged on the dead and hovered around the living. Undaunted for over five hundred millenniums, these primitive creatures made light of the terrible shot and shell, danced nimbly around whizzing fragments of shrapnel and flirted with the belching muzzles of cannon. Only the napalm staggered them. Thousands died in the crackling orange splashes. Only to be replaced by endless thousands more. If one wanted to be intimate with all the horrors of a battlefield, one need be but an insect. Could he make a *haiku* of that? Asiro Tachikawa wondered.

"We're doing our best," the First Cohort executive officer, Maj. Bill "Poet" DeVere, cut through his commander's entomological reflections.

"I know that. The Sandinistas have gotten word that our reinforcements are on the way. They'll do everything they can to punch through before we are strong enough to counterattack. Inform Captains Black and Dyer to move their Centuries into position to support the artillery. The next two or three hours are going to be critical."

"Right away, sir," DeVere responded.

"How's Cepeda and his Bushman contingent doing?" Tachikawa inquired, settling on a not-too-certain diversionary move he had planned.

"Fine, far as I know. If anyone can find the proof we need, Juan Cepeda can. He's overdue reporting in now. I'll let you know when something breaks. Now, ammo supply for the G-Six guns . . ."

Oh, yes, Tachikawa thought. Those South African One-five-fives were superlative artillery, but they ate a whale of a lot. If they lost any of them, they'd really be done for.

"Baltimore, this is Cherokee Three Point Two. Baltimore, this is Cherokee Three Point Two. Do you copy?" Maj. Juan Jose Cepeda, a former Contra and now Jay Solice's deputy G-2, wiped sweat from his brow and keyed the mike again. "Baltimore, this is Cherokee Three."

"Roger, Cherokee Three. We have you. Report, over."

"Baltimore, we have visual contact with the subjects in question. Verify that the India Bravo is here. By count, nearly intact. We are at grid one-two-Golf, coordinates eight-five-zero-seven by one-one-zero-seven. The big Sierra is here now. They are not 'chasing,' or 'attacking.' They appear to have joined up, I say again, joined up with India Bravo and are attacking settlements in the northern Departments."

"There is no conflict? Over."

"Negative, Baltimore. No conflict."

"Are they able to join the main Sierra force on the highway?"

"Roger that. But it will take a while. They have to cross the flood plain of the San Carlos River and the river itself. If we implement Plan Oscar, they can be delayed at least a day. Over."

Poet DeVere gave a significant glance to Asiro Tachikawa. "There's the good news."

Lt. Col. Tachikawa took the mike. "That big earthen dam at the headwaters is the key." He pressed the talk button. "Cherokee three, this is Baltimore zero-zero. Activate Plan Oscar. I say again, activate Oscar."

* * *

"Dik-Dik, this is Simba, what is your ETA? Over." The large, handsome black man who spoke into the mike aboard the Huey slick had a polished Oxford accent with only a slight hint of Matabele attached. He worked hard at downplaying his speech pattern when communicating with Lt. Able and his Bushmen.

"Simba, this Dik-Dik. We hear you five on. Be dis folk big coolee soon now. Walk-around two finger of sun, mebbe."

Sanford Motubu winced. Even after the intensive English lessons at Corsair Cay, the Bushmen spoke their own variety of Pidgin, to the exclusion of all proper form. "Roger, Dik-Dik. Keep this fellow channel open, yes?"

"Dik-Dik do."

According to plan, the Bushmen would secure the dam, if indeed that need be done. Motubu would come in with a load of slow-burning, earth-moving explosives in the Huey and see to their deployment. When the charges were ready, Able and his Bushmen would leave the area with all haste. The chopper would lift off and, when Able and his crew had reached a safe distance, the dam would be blown. Since the crossing point for the International Brigade was so far below the dam, with the floodplain so wide, there was little hope the resultant flood would be particularly lethal to the enemy. Worst scenario had them slowed, perhaps turned back. At best, the International Brigade and the Sandinista strike force would lose a lot of equipment, have hardships aplenty, and be destroyed as an effective fighting force. Sanford Motubu weighed it all again.

"Simba, this Dik-Dik. We be at that place. Ov'ah."

"Alright, take her on in. Simba out." He paused a moment, frowning. "Be a good chap and let's scout it a bit first. Able's idea of a good, safe place might not be the same as ours, eh?" Motubu told the Legion pilot.

They landed and quickly set to preparing the charges. A huge bundle of explosives was rigged and lowered on the wet side of the dam. It would be fired an eighth of a second behind a corresponding sextet of forty-pound shaped charges on the dry side. Each of these would be positioned at the optimum penetration standoff. When all was in readiness, Sanford Mobutu waved to Lt. Able.

"Alright, Able. Take 'em out fast now. We make radio check every two fingers of sun, hey?"

Ten minutes later the Huey lifted off. Simba called Dik-Dik. The Bushmen were running fast, away from the dam at a ninety-degree angle. Ten minutes after that, at a higher angle, Motubu spotted them emerging from trees and crossing a clearing.

"Simba, this Dik-Dik. We see you. All good run-run now," Lt. Able reported.

"Carry on," the big black man replied, feeling foolish for saying it.

At thirty minutes after departure, Motubu made a final contact. "We're firing now," he concluded.

Sanford Motubu pressed the red button on the radio detonator at one side, lashed to a frame member. At once he craned to look out the open door. At first it appeared that the attempt had failed. Smoky bubbles rose behind the dam. A light breeze blew away six columns of dust from the face, leaving nothing impressive behind. Then a thin trickle of water appeared on the outer curve of the dam. Steadily it widened, became a spurting stream, the thickness of a man's arm. The hole in the loosened dirt began to enlarge at an ever-increasing rate.

Then, in a sudden rush of flying mud and hurtling water, the damaged central span was carried away. A wall of foaming brown toppled to the riverbed below the dam. With a roar, the rest of the obstruction melted and swirled off behind the huge flood crest.

"A job well done, I'd say," Sanford Motubu congratulated himself. Downriver, the Sandinistas would soon learn of his diligence, he thought with pride.

Watching the one-sided air battle as the Air Force transport planes settled in with the final Cohort, Gen. Watie was jubilant. The Sandinistas had thrown every aircraft they had into this attempt to deny reinforcements to the Legion. With the added strength of Legion AA batteries already being deployed, this attack by enemy fighters was even more suicidal than before. When the last C-5's wheels touched the ground, Watie told his driver to take him to the open pavilion where the officers had been instructed to assemble.

"Gentlemen, time is too precious for me to waste a lot of time on words," Gen. Watie informed them. "Welcome to Costa Rica. You are to deploy your men immediately and prepare for battle. All armor will be massed under Lt. Colonel Rounding, and placed in defilade position behind the passes into the San José Basin. That will require a movement of some thirty-five klicks north of here. Your mission is to deny access to the basin to the Nicaraguan forces. Second, Third and Fourth Cohorts will provide infantry and artillery support to the blocking force. Fifth Cohort, our new Dragoons, will be carried into battle, where needed, by the replacement APCs, which came overland from Limón."

Watie paused for a moment and stared off toward the dark shapes of the mountains. "We are being sorely misused in this sort of static defense and I anticipate casualties in excess of the norm. Unfortunately, until the enemy thrust develops, and we can devise a means of breaking it, we cannot go on the offensive and exploit any breakthrough we achieve. Once we do, and given that I have my way about it, we're going balls-to-the-wall, all the way to Managua."

Gen. Watie hadn't expected a rousing cheer, but he got one.

Brigadier General Laslo Bartonachek hated insects. Compared to this pestiferous jungle, there were so few in his native Czechoslovakia that one could hardly notice them. He, and his Nicaraguan counterpart, *Comandante de Brigada* Carlos Maria Merida, stumbled through the lush undergrowth on paths newly cut by their "recruited" Costa Rican conscripts. Why had he chosen to accept assignment as commander of the International Brigade? He'd had a choice, Bartonachek reflected. He could have gone to North Africa and worked as an advisor in Khaddafi's terrorist schools. Instead he wound up in this rotten jungle.

"We've become immune to the smells," Gen. Bartonachek confided to Comandante Merida. "Yet these infernal insects still can drive men mad."

"Oh, there's more to come, General," Merida advised him. "Now that we're in the lowlands, which flood every rainy season, we can look forward to leeches, and the diseases they cause."

"You're so full of hope," Bartonachek growled.

"Point squad for you, sir," the RTO informed Bartonachek.

"What is it?" the Czech general growled.

"We've broken out onto the flats, sir," came the reply. "There's clumps of sawgrass higher than our heads in places, but we can see the sunlight off the San Carlos River in the distance ahead."

"Thank you, Red Fern. Continue the advance, and mark the trail. Keep a sharp eye for any enemy activity. Red Star, out." To the Sandinista officer he snarled, "Sawgrass. What next?"

"I forgot to mention that, I suppose. At least it's a change from the jungle."

"Ummm. I've seen webbing gear cut by sawgrass in Southeast Asia," Bartonachek remarked. "Tropical jungle is all alike. A steam pressure cooker that saps men's strength in minutes and leaves them dizzy and disoriented when it comes time to fight. Except for those who were born there," he amended.

"True enough. Which hardly leaves one's troops ready to face the sun beating down on sawgrass fields at forty-nine degrees, provided you can find shade for the thermometer, and ninety-eight percent humidity."

"Any temperature over twenty-five Celsius is too hot for me," Bartonachek observed.

"Ah, you Europeans. You're spoiled. And lucky. What the Americans call seventy-five degrees is our winter temperature. If we had a climate like that we'd get twice the work out of our laborers."

"You forget the seven or so months of sub-zero winter," Bartonachek riposted. "Ach, this talk of weather is too much for me. All the same, the men are going to be so worn out after negotiating all this that they'll make better candidates for hospital than battle, by the time we reach the Central Highlands."

"I don't want to admit it, but I'm afraid you're right. We'll need at least a full day's rest," Comandante Merida agreed.

"But, will the Legion give us that time?" Gen. Bartonachek asked rhetorically.

The RTO had the handset ready again. "Red Fern, sir."

"Go ahead," Bartonachek snapped.

"We're making slow progress, sir. This is better country for airboats. From the looks of it, the sawgrass plain extends beyond the river to some hilly jungle. Beyond that's the mountain pass. There's more water than we were told to expect, too, sir."

"How long do you estimate to the river? Over."

"Maybe two hours. We're barely making three kilometers an hour, sir."

"Keep going. Report back when you reach the riverbank. Red Star, out."

Under the blistering punishment of the sun and the slashing revenge of the sawgrass, an hour and forty minutes went miserably by. The point called again.

"Red Star, we're at the river. It's running exceedingly high and swiftly, sir. Looks like it's rising. Crossing's going to be difficult. Over."

"Spread out and look for a place to ford, Red Fern. If necessary find two places. We have a lot of people to get across. Red Star, out."

Gen. Bartonachek returned the handset only to receive another. "El Castillo Base, General. They have an aerial recon report."

"Red Star, this is El Castillo," a tinny voice rattled the ear piece diaphragm. "Be advised that high-level recon reports the San Carlos dam has been ruptured. A catastrophically high floodcrest has devastated the upper reaches of the river and continues to move your direction. Estimates predict a two- to three-meter wall of water will inundate the floodplain in a matter of minutes."

The two generals exchanged horrified expressions.

"You heard that," Bartonachek said in a strangled voice. A statement, not a question.

"We've got to get moving at once. Call back the point from the river. Find anything, any high ground," Merida recited anxiously. He grabbed the other radio, while the Czechoslovak officer extracted more information from the Nicaraguan base.

While their officers shouted, the nearest men began to struggle with the stubborn crew-served weapons. Low hummocks that supported a few pine trees being the only high ground, the first men to reach them began to point frantically to the west. Kilometers wide, and frothing around obstacles, the three-meter crest rushed toward them. Men yelled in frantic disorganization as the restive water ahead of the flood rose to waist deep. All who could reached the low hillocks, which were too small and too far apart to accommodate everyone. With the force of a powerful explosion the foaming wall of liquid burst over the International Brigade and the Sandinista contingent.

In an instant, many of the men were bowled over and drowned. Most of the more fortunate lost their personal weapons and rations. None save those who reached the higher ground could survive. And those soon found themselves barely able to stand against the swift current of chest-high water. More heads than human bobbed in the water.

Mountain lions, snakes, and jaguars found their curt tempers even shorter when puny little men blocked their way to the trees and safety. Instinctively they lashed out. Blood in the water triggered a feeding frenzy among the frightened and dislocated crocs. Once the terrible crest had passed, Gen. Bartonachek located his radio operator and contacted the operations base.

"There is some good news, Red Star," the reply came. "The weather people and engineers in Managua predict that the waters will recede within twenty-four hours."

"By then, we'll be lucky if we have a third of our force left," Bartonachek confided to Comandante Merida.

CHAPTER
15

Steel or not, Commodore Stan McDade was ready to chew the rail off the starboard side of the flying bridge of the *Scipio Africanus*. "Those miserable ingrate bastards," he growled aloud.

For the past ten hours the Panamanian-run Canal Authority had refused to recognize his War Priority. It would, they smugly estimated, take another seventy-two hours before they began locking the Legion Fleet through the canal. A pilot shortage, they explained. Also, many others were in line long before they arrived. Much against his own inclinations—"Why give the bastards any more of our money than we need to?"—he at last went inside the pilothouse to issue new orders.

"Attention in the Task Force," he spoke over the general command net. "Liberty is hereby authorized for all qualified personnel. Liberty will be in two sections, port and starboard, according to berthing arrangements. Liberty boats to stand by the gangways at eleven-thirty hours. All liberty to be for twenty-four hours only. That is all."

"You, ah, are certainly being, ah, *generous*," the cold voice of Admiral O'Fallon grated from behind Commodore McDade. "Hardly the way to run tight ships."

"Thank you for your Regular Navy advice, Admiral,"

Stan said lightly. "We also have ninety-eight-degree temperature and one hundred percent humidity. Also, need I remind you, several thousand of the meanest sons of bitches in the world confined below decks. Better they take out their frustrations on the Panamanians than each other."

"They could be chipping and scraping, repainting," O'Fallon offered.

"It's already done. Three times. Twice while you were commanding the training force and once on the way down here. There's nothing left to chip, scrape, or paint. All brass is polished and the other bright work treated with semichrome. There's been three inspections in five days. All dungarees have been starched and I'm sure that if you rubbed one of the deck hands, he'd squeak. I don't know much about the Navy, Admiral, but on the inner-island schooners I'm familiar with a 'tight ship' meant high morale, not a lot of chickenshit make-do work for the crew."

"Even if this is an independent command, Naval regulations should be maintained at all cost, and at all times," O'Fallon sniffed. "The Pentagon will have to be notified of this deviation."

"You agree that this delay is deliberate, to foul our schedule?" McDade snapped.

"Well, ah, yes. Of course. It certainly seems that way," O'Fallon staggered.

"Well then, when several thousand Legionnaires descend on an unsuspecting Colon, I'm betting pressure will be put on to move us through with considerably more dispatch," Stan said through a grin.

Even the sour Thomas O'Fallon developed a fleeting smile. "You are a devious one, Commodore McDade."

"Why, thank you, Admiral. Will you join me ashore for a drink?" Stan offered.

"I, ah, think I'll accept, Commodore. Provided we get the opportunity to observe the natives being terrorized by your Legionnaires."

Legion sailors swarmed into Colon. American dollars in Legion hands were spent with all the ease of any other currency in the international free port. At first the authorities treated the arrival of the Legion like some sort of infestation. Police patrols doubled, then tripled. The helmeted officers went about with stormy expressions that clearly announced their eagerness to bust some Legion heads. Word immediately spread that the Heroes of Panama had returned.

"Our comrades are dying in battle down in Costa Rica," one Master Sergeant Gunner's Mate complained loudly in a stevedore's bar along the wharf. "It's not bad enough they're facing the Sandinista army, your thrice-cursed Panamanian bureaucrats are holding up our passage through the canal."

Mindful of their years of subjugation under Gen. Noriega, and their recent liberation by the direct intervention of the American Foreign Legion, the people reacted with open hearts and unbounded gratitude. In the entire city of Colon not a Legionnaire could spend money on liquor or women, though both flowed in ample quantities. The more the people heard of the ingratitude of their government, the more they doubted its decision-making abilities. While the Legionnaires feasted, drank, danced, and screwed their way into happy oblivion, the citizens of Panama decided they had to once more take charge of matters for themselves.

By early morning, a silent mob of working-class Panamanians blocked the land access to the canal. They stood about quietly, not even raising their voices when they cursed the bureaucrats and the soldiers sent to disperse them. Hung-over Legionnaires returning to the ships were cheered heartily and given presents of liquor, flowers, roasted chickens, suckling pigs, and lingering, passionate kisses. By ten o'clock, letters and telephone calls began to flood into the government offices. Still the workers remained in surly knots around the gates into the Zone.

Stung by their own citizens' accusations that they had betrayed Latin hospitality, and would dare, in light of past events, to collaborate with the Nicaraguans, the officials began, snail-like, to move. By noon, all liberties had been canceled and the *Scipio* began nudging her way into Gatun

Lock. Jubilant crowds gathered to throw flowers and cheer on the fleet.

"Although there is no reason given for the abrupt change in policy," Peter Jennings's voice, heavy with regret, told the ABC television audience, "the Canal Company, under urging from the Panamanian government, has announced that it will recognize the Wartime Priority of the Liberty Corps. The mercenary warships are moving through the locks at this time. Additional disturbing news comes from the capital of Panama. The mayor of Panama City has announced that he wishes to express his constituents' gratitude to the Legion for the nineteen ninety-nine liberation of the country, and has requested permission to board the Legion flagship, the *Scipio Africanus*, to do so. At the Legion recruiting offices in Panama, it is reported that droves of would-be volunteers are being turned away. A reliable source informed ABC News that this is not the case. The hordes of people descending on the Legion recruiting stations are irate protesters, bent upon demonstrating against the Legion presence in their country and the danger of Legion warships menacing them from the Canal. We'll have a follow-up on that on the Evening News at six o'clock. Elsewhere . . ."

"Isn't that a crock of shit," Lt. Col. Sam Seagraves declared as he turned away from the *Scipio*'s wardroom satellite television set.

"The reason they won't show it now," Maj. John Lowe, Engineering Division and Task Force historian, opined, "is that it will probably take them until six New York time to hire some 'demonstrators' and have placards printed for them."

"From what we got over the secure line from the recruiting office in Colon," Sam went on, "there are Panamanian army officers willing to take private's rank to get into the Legion."

"Once we're clear of the Canal and in Costa Rican waters, we can rattle a few Nicaraguan cages and see what

Peter Perfect there has to say about that," the Flight Operations officer suggested.

Bitter regret clear on his face, Asiro Tachikawa gave the order for the First Cohort to break contact and evacuate the final pass between the advancing Sandinistas and the San José Basin. Although the other Cohorts had arrived in-country, they had not had time to deploy as yet and provide effective resistance. Buying time, he would have to console himself with the thought that this withdrawal purchased precious hours for Norm Watie to take up positions to flatten the on-rushing Sandinista menace.

"Legion Golf will provide transportation," he went on, reading the order. "Legion Kilo is to provide heavy support during the withdrawal, along with Delta of the First, who will be the rear guard. That's all, gentlemen. Unless you have serious questions, please get to it, we want to minimize casualties."

Legion Golf's trucks spread out along the front with surprising speed. With the surviving troops aboard, Golf's drivers sped along the Pan American Highway toward San José. Behind them, the Legion artillery fell silent. Flashing through the sky, the Merlins of Legion Kilo set off to harry the Sandinista forces as they formed up to make rapid pursuit. The guns and rockets of Legion Lima opened up, sending more shards of Legion steel into the ranks of the enemy. Confusion developed and, with it, the inevitable delay. Delta of the First emptied its salvos and began to break down.

First to depart were the 4.2 mortars. Then the towed artillery evacuated. Last to abandon their positions were the long-range South African G-6, 155s. Covering their withdrawal, the Merlins kept the Nicaraguan heads low. There were no cheers at this troop movement. On every palate lay the bitter bile of running from the enemy.

"They are gone," a smiling captain announced over the bustle of the headquarters command vehicle. "Our forward elements are at the crest of the pass. They report not a single Legion element within effective range. They're all heading to San José, like whipped curs."

"Excellent," Comandante Hector Boaz barked. "Only, where are our comrades under Carlos Merida? And where's Bartonachek's International Brigade? They were to link up with us before the final thrust. In twelve hours, Costa Rica could be ours."

"They are coming, Comrade Comandante," Subcomandante Jaime Navarre answered. "They have been delayed by the flooding after the infernal Legion blew up the Rio San Carlos dam."

"Humm. Send the point unit down the slopes, to follow the Legion. Our advance elements should move out at once."

"Immediately, Comrade Comandante," Navarre assured him.

Three companies of tanks, mostly older T-72s, spearheaded the advance. Behind them came long columns of armored personnel carriers with the motorized infantry. Artillery trains formed up and sped off. Progress went well. Until a sudden confusion of loud blasts ended the rapid advance.

Sewn by Merlin 2000s, the tiny MIFF mines had waited unseen, their sensitive antennas straining to hear the desired vibrations from enemy armor and APCs. Once detected, the nasty little devices waited until a vehicle was directly overhead, and detonated. Seven MBTs and eleven APCs erupted and sent their passengers off to Red oblivion.

"Mines, mines, mines," the call jammed the airwaves.

The pesky submunitions demanded long, careful attention to render them ineffective. Every minute that ticked by increased Comandante Boaz's impatience. At last a free zone was established and the column started off.

"I find it difficult to believe that this Legion defeated our troops in Panama last year," Comandante Boaz remarked an hour later, as the advance elements of one Motorized Rifle Division deployed to form a defensive perimeter in the great, verdant farmland of the San José Basin.

"There they had the initiative, the element of surprise, and our limited maneuvering area on their side," Comandante (Col.) Ronpope, the division commander, replied. "Here we have the initiative and ample space."

"Which we shall exploit," Boaz acknowledged. "The moment your lead elements have established a perimeter, be ready to move the remainder of your division, and that of Arturo Vega, through the lines. We must move swiftly while we can."

Soon the ominous horde of two Soviet-style Motorized Rifle Divisions fanned out on the open country. Blasting deserted homes and farmsteads that might serve as observation posts, their heavy tank elements slashed through fences and across peaceful fields of crops. No hand was raised against them as they leapfrogged across country. Battle lines formed, dissolved, and reformed while supply trucks began the lengthy task of topping off depleted tanks and ammo racks. It all began to seem too easy.

Until, from the direction of far-off San José, a great cloud of dust and diesel fumes began to rise. The air shuddered to the freight train rumble of incoming rounds. To sit still was to die. Knowing this, the Sandinista commanders ordered an all-out assault, to get inside the expected rain of artillery shells.

Their commands came too late, as the first Legion destruction burst among them. With unerring accuracy, the Copperhead missiles, fired by the Legion 155s, homed in on T-72 tanks. Guided by laser target designators left by Lt. Col. Tachikawa in the mountains behind the invader, the deadly projectiles fell like celestial chastisement. Dust, smoke, and flame obscured the Sandinista front as one in every three tanks became a victim.

There had to be a certain sort of heaven for a born tanker. Lt. Col. Gordon Rounding could expect nothing finer in the afterlife. He bet on it solidly as his command Stingray Commando's bow began to settle onto an even keel. Recovering from the torque of acceleration, it slammed toward a distant enemy, marked only by a growing number of oily smoke columns on the horizon. Another bloody irregularity in the terrain, he thought, and they'd all be into a Number 10 Excedrin headache. Yet, they had to proceed at all possible haste. At the rate the artillery was scoring . . .

"Give it some more throttle," he shouted over the intercom. "We've got to get there quickly or there won't be anything left to shoot at."

A shadow drew his attention to a swarm of Merlins passing overhead. The Sandinistas would have their MiGs up. For two days Daniel Ortega had been squealing like a pig on the more than obliging world media about the violation of airspace by "criminal hooligans" of the mercenary Foreign Legion. Though Ortega, and the newsmen, failed to mention that the airspace in question belonged to Costa Rica, not Nicaragua. Gordon studied the sky a moment longer, which gave him an excellent view of a high-altitude, cartwheeling fireball.

"Lovely, lovely. I bid you a fond adieu," he said aloud to yet another Red jet jockey.

CHAPTER
16

"Exposure! Hell, there's not a damned thing wrong with me that Becky couldn't cure," an exasperated Captain Jim Levin shouted at the young executive officer.

Still angry at the Navy because the captain of the rescue ship had given orders to blow his precious Merlin out of the water, Arizona Jim found cause for grievance everywhere. Fortunately, the officer in question had issued his order before moving his ship away. Jim had leaped over the rail and refused rescue until Lt. Commander Pieper had agreed to sway the craft aboard. Jim had stayed with Becky and had personally set the hook in the "Lift Here" pad-eye, fitted in the weapons compartment. He continued to refuse treatment when the Navy demo man reluctantly came down to help cut away the jammed missile. Then, with that completed, Jim climbed into the cockpit for the ride up.

Even when safely on deck, Jim wouldn't report to Sick Bay until the OOD (Officer of the Deck) promised the order had been rescinded. Then he had submitted to a cursory examination, received fresh, dry clothing, and slept the clock around. Ten minutes after awakening the Executive Officer came to inform him that the captain had graciously dropped charges, which ranged from mutiny and insubordination to conduct unbecoming an officer, and that when the ship's surgeon released him, Jim would be welcome in the officers' wardroom. After, of course, a thorough physical examination. That's when Jim blew his stack the second time.

"Becky? Who's that?" the XO inquired.

"My bird's computer," Arizona Jim responded. "So I swallowed a little seawater, I got a headache and red eyes. Even the most simpleminded computer could prescribe for that."

"Won't do, though," the Executive Officer said cheerily. "Got to follow Regulations. The reputation of the entire U.S. Caribbean patrol squadron is at stake."

"Hurrumph! Big deal," Capt. Levin grumbled. "Right damn now, the Legion will be kicking ass and my own squadron right in the middle of it, while Becky and I are cruising the romantic Caribbean with a ship full of swab jockeys."

The young exec bridled a bit at that description, yet remained calm. "Just go see the Doc, eh? Then come on up and have coffee and gossip with the rest of us. We're all anxious to hear what a real fighting force is doing."

Flattery, eh? Well, Arizona Jim decided in favor of going along; the Legion didn't promise there would *always* be justice. Maybe a little sincere hero worship would soothe ragged nerve ends.

A strong feeling of *dejà vu* assailed Captain Mark McDade as his Merlin 2000-A flashed toward Sandinista lines. It was not a comfortable sensation. The last time he'd done this it had ended with a spectacular crash when he'd inadvertently shot himself down. Combine that with getting blown out of the air when Spetsnaz destroyed the barge on which his flight was practicing carrier landings, and it added up to two strikes against him.

Three strikes and you're out.

The thought wouldn't shake out of Mark's head. Ahead of him, the swarm of Merlin 400s streaked over Legion Charley as the line of Cadillac Gage Stingrays reared the muzzles of their 105mm L-5 guns toward the sky in a jackrabbit start that would do credit to a funny car. The wheeled APCs began to follow, right on their tails. At the reduced speed of 400 mph, to allow the 400 models time to suppress AA fire, Mark and his flight skimmed over the San José Basin at 50 feet off the ground. The air went suddenly hazy from smoke and dust. Gradually emerging, Mark saw the bulk of a T-72 in his HUD.

A gentle flex of the wrist, and twitch of his right thumb, slammed one of his six Javelin missiles into the turret ring. Mark banked hard right as troops ran every way through the smog of battle in an attempt to get clear of blazing APCs left from the earlier bombardment and the strike of the little birds. Mark located another MBT and lined up on it.

Three bullets struck the Lexan canopy, bracketing his head and causing a flinch that jerked the Javelin off target. A quick check verified for Mark that many of the Sandinista foot soldiers had rallied and were pouring a concentrated small arms fire on the predatory birds. Time to end such unpleasantries.

"Barbarian flight, this is Barbarian Zero-zero. Come to one-two angels at once, and orbit. We'll let the peewees do what they do best."

With breath-taking airshow precision, the A models pulled out and up. They swiftly disengaged the tanks and personnel carriers and made way for the little 400s to slash in with their 30mm cannon blazing. With their bigger brothers watching from above, the sprightly birds tangled with their ground objectives. Here and there one of them made a 3.5 run on a still-operational APC. These they trashed with minimal effort. After a couple of passes, Mark observed that the MBTs were pulling away from the embattled infantry.

"Barbarians, let's go down and make a flanking run on those tanks," he commanded. "Fifteen-second intervals, keep it tight."

Nose down, the powerful 2000-A under Mark's command roared toward the Sandinista armor. Mark unleashed his remaining four Javelins as rapidly as he could acquire targets. When the last one ignited and hurtled toward a rendezvous with a T-72, Mark pulled up to assess the damage.

The killing ground looked like a plain in Hell. By the time all sixteen of his Merlins had expended their 96 missiles, the Sandinista armor force had been cut in half and the remainder could see the battle line of Stingrays on the horizon, closing fast.

"Lookin' good, Barbarians. Let's head for the barn. These nags need to eat," Mark ordered cheerily.

Gordon Rounding's worst fears were being realized. There'd be no climactic clash of steel brutes. No triumphant ride into a tanker's Valhalla, with Georgie Patton on hand to greet them. The surviving Sandinista T-72s fired one round each, then turned tail and ran. He had no trouble visualizing what would happen when the panic-stricken drivers hit the bottleneck of the pass. The chaos would be perfect for the blasted Merlins.

Sitting high in his command cupola, Gordon shook a fist at the last sleek little Merlin as it streaked back for replenishment at San José. The Legion armor commander knew full well the inexpensive little craft had doomed to oblivion any future massive battles between multimillion-dollar iron monsters. Sighing heavily, he spoke his thoughts to his crew.

"It's the end of an era, lads. From now on, you and I, we're all as obsolete as the bloody dinosaur."

Major Pavel Shchevko of the KGB was appalled. He had been assigned to observe a triumph of Soviet equipment and tactics and to make a glowing report on its success. Instead he had witnessed a debacle. Two Motorized Infantry Divisions had been destroyed before his very eyes. Worse, it had happened before they could even get their superior weapons into action. Had Ortega been a sublime fool? And had his own superiors been blithely led down a path to discredit and ridicule? Still, there remained a final gambit.

Fortunately, the Sandinistas had been ordered to hold

their Hokum gunships in reserve. They had been located far enough from the battle that an improperly indoctrinated pilot could not claim the million-dollar reward from the Legion. Soviet command in Managua had released the three-hundred-mile-per-hour, counter-rotating, twin main rotor choppers at his request the moment he realized the assault was in trouble.

They were still a goodly hour out. In the meantime, he had to do something to prevent all-out hysteria among the troops. At a momentary slowdown, he darted from his rolling vehicle to that of the Nicaraguan CO. He yanked the external telephone from its small box and shouted into it. No response. Next he drew his Makarov pistol and banged on the personnel hatch at the rear. When it opened he stepped inside.

"What is it, Major?" the harried Sandinista demanded testily.

"Comandante Boaz, you are relieved of your command. Confine yourself in my command vehicle until two of my men can be released to escort you to Managua."

Arctic ice could not have chilled Comandante Boaz more. He stammered and literally wrung his hands. His eyes had a haunted look, he tried to stand fast.

"You do as I order or shall I shoot you down here myself," Shchevko demanded.

"My men wouldn't let you. You are in a-an army of loyal N-Nicaraguans," Boaz bleated.

"I am in an army of *good communists*," Shchevko snapped. "You two, take the Comandante to my vehicle at once."

"Yes, Comrade Major," the nearest Nicaraguan responded in a monotone.

After the deposed officer had departed, Shchevko demanded a report on the situation, then rubbed his hands eagerly. "Now, let's see what we can do to prevent a traffic jam at the pass." He spoke to the radio operators. "Order the right and left flanks to fall back and concentrate on the center. They are to dismount their troops and form a defensive perimeter. Antitank missiles are to receive primary consideration. All turreted vehicles in this command are to reverse turrets and lay down concentrated fire to our rear."

From his position on the mountainside to the north of the pass, Col. Mark Kelly got on the radio to Capt. Jesus Bustamante Pavlov Garcia. He spoke crisply to the young officer from the White Russian colony outside Ensenada, Baja California, ticking off assignments from memory.

"You are to seal the pass with Grim-Twenty rounds from your four-point-twos. Fire will be called for you by Kiowa Six. Closer in, use your light one-oh-fives to paste hell out of the retreating Sandinista forces. Fire control will be your own, Tonkawa One."

"Roger, Modoc. The choppers just delivered the last of my British light guns. It'll take a few rounds to register it. Over."

Mark considered for a moment. Third Cohort would be doing the same thing on the south side, except for the added assignment of blocking the pass. That should provide enough firepower to keep the Nicaraguans off balance. A quick check through his binoculars revealed Legions Charley, Hotel, India, and Lima charging across the basin in the distance. They'd be nipping at the heels of the retreating enemy in a matter of minutes.

"Okay, Tonkawa One, shoot in that gun and be ready for individual fire missions or Century fire calls within ten minutes. Modoc Zero-zero out." Mark keyed another frequency and spoke briskly. "Kiowa Six, this is Modoc Zero-zero. Over."

"Gotcha, Modoc Zero-zero," Lt. Bill Kane responded.

"Kiowa Six, you'd best stand by to designate targets and call down smart rounds on your eleven o'clock. You'll give fire missions to Tonkawa Four starting now. There's a bunch of T-Seventy-twos making a run for the pass. Try to block the entrance to the pass with knocked-out tanks so the others will be forced to surrender." The Legion had been trashing entirely too much equipment so far on this operation, Mark knew. "Don't lock your transmit open, because Tonkawa Six will be giving fire missions on the same frequency. Modoc Zero-zero, out."

Lt. Col. Kelly took time to grab a gulp of lukewarm coffee, grimaced and keyed his mike again. "Shoshoni One, Blackhawk One, Kiowa One, this is Modoc Zero-zero," he summoned Captains Harlan "Alkey" Seltzer, Lloyd "Bud" Harshman, and George "Tex" Ade. "Move down the mountain and hit the Sandinistas in the flank. This is the big one, boys. Kick some Red ass."

Doggies if it didn't feel a whole lot different, walkin' into a fight, instead of powered up on a jet ski or a small boat. Lt. Don Hoover made a quick visual check of his platoon and squared his shoulders. Hell of a thing, he considered. A fellow'd think these Central Americans would work hard at getting along with each other. Yet, here was the Legion trying to keep one pipsqueak country from kicking crap out of another pipsqueak country. He hadn't read much about the Sandinistas and Nicaragua, or Costa Rica for that matter. He hadn't read much of anything, except gun magazines, until he joined the Legion. From what he could see, their flanking movement was turning into an assault on the Sandinista rear. A 7.62 × 39 slug cracked past Don's crested helmet.

"Shit! Heads up, guys, these jerks shoot better than those fuzzy-wuzzies down in the South Pacific," he cautioned his troops.

"They're breakin', Loo," Sgt. Anderson announced from the far end of the skirmish line. A replacement for Frank Miner, who'd bought it on New Caledonia, Chris Anderson was working out fine as a platoon sergeant. "Jeez, they're runnin' like antelope. We're right in among their field kitchen trucks."

"Fix glaudii," Lt. Hoover snapped, attaching his Legion bayonet. "We're gonna roll those muthers up on their MLR."

It seemed like a surrealist dream. Frightened Mestizo faces popped up, only to fall away, hugging the ground, hands clasped over necks. Others tried to tough it out. The silent jar of contact, parry, thrust, counter, thrust again. The mouths working, silent words of pain that would never be heard as gouts of blood spilled over stretched lips. Twist and yank, stumble forward, eyes wild. Another enemy, this one shrieking as he ran forward, a machete raised. Lt. Hoover shot him between the eyes. Stomach queasy with the rich, coppery smell of gore. Arms heavy now, tired of the unaccustomed exercise.

Did it feel like this when they harvested wheat with a scythe? Green uniforms showed everywhere. Men surrounded, others ran, some whimpered. Faces twisted in pain and fear as Sandinistas died in extreme agony from the glaudii, the leaf-shaped Legion steel, in their guts. Blood began to dry and cake on his hands and uniform. Lt. Don Hoover found himself floating in a gray haze of fatigue, red-tinged with the life sap of the enemy. A clear space . . . emptiness . . . no one left to butt-stroke and stick, none to fend off.

Awed, as though by a solemn, spiritual experience, Lt. Don Hoover and the Legionnaires around him sank to the ground. "Shit," their platoon leader said almost reverently. "Awh, shit, that was somethin'."

Invisible laser spots targeted the hapless armor. "Tonkawa Four, I have a fire mission. Send six Smart rounds, TOT three-zero seconds. Over."

"Rog, Kiowa Six. On their way," the acknowledgment rattled in Bill Kane's helmet speaker.

Five of the six T-72s died in a true holocaust thirty seconds later. Bill keyed his mike. "Tonkawa Four, we have spots on more armor than you have time to shoot. Bring in the Grims."

"Roger, Kiowa Six. We copy free fire, I say again, free fire. Over."

"You got it, Tonkawa Four." Lt. Bill Kane wiped sweat from his face. How could it be so friggin' hot in the mountains? Movement drew his attention to one side.

Quickly Kane triggered off a short burst from his GAS at four figures leapfrogging through the rocks. Two went down. At least these Sandinistas had their shit together, he thought. They want to silence this radio and know how to go about it. Their whole fighting stance had changed. It was like maybe the same people were no longer commanding. Smashed and burning tanks now closed the wide road that led into the pass. Enough junk and bodies lay about to clog the treads of any vehicle that tried to force a path through the carnage. He saw the small spheroid of the Soviet grenade poised at the top of its arc.

Ducking low into his boulder patch, Kane left his mouth open and squeezed eyes tightly shut. Even with ear protectors the blast left him groggy, a wild ringing inside his head. Steel balls sang off the rocks and chips of volcanic refuse cut and stung his cheeks. No time to crybaby. Bill popped up and cut off a three-round burst with his Garris Assault Rifle. One Sandinista went down. The other threw away his AKS and raised trembling arms above his head. The platoon net spluttered in his ear.

"Say again, I lost you to an M-Ten. Over."

"They're givin' up, Loo," one of his squad leaders informed Bill. Voice tone was meaningless.

"Who is that?" Kane demanded.

"Inca Three, Kiowa Six. They're all givin' up."

"That don't mean the rest of 'em will," Kane cautioned. "Form up and we'll herd the prisoners ahead of us down the slope to the road. Looks like the pass is ours."

CHAPTER
17

Gray-brown dust from crushed concrete rooster-tailed behind the speeding armor of Gordon Rounding's Legion Hotel. Eager for a battle, eyes gorged with internal pressure, the Legion tankers' bellicose expressions changed to ones of consternation the closer they came to the pass. When they reached Capt. Harshman and Lt. Hoover, the encounter might have been a replay of Montgomery's triumphant entry into Messina, Sicily, only to find Georgie Patton there to greet him. Although he put forth a good face on it all, Gordon Rounding was heartbroken. The battle was over and his beloved Commando Stingrays had not fired a shot. While the three officers surveyed the destruction, the Legion command net came to life.

"This is Cherokee Zero-zero." Swiftly Gen. Watie gave orders for the battle area to be secured and the pass to be cleared. He also had special orders for Rounding. "You'll move out immediately through the pass and head for Puntarenas on the Gulf of Nicoya. Cherokee Zero-zero, out."

That left Harshman and Hoover with hundreds of Sandinista prisoners. With battle fever ebbing and the elation of victory subsiding, the officers and their men found themselves in a tired numbness. They went mechanically about clearing the road. Burned-out hulks got shoved aside without even a ragged cheer. In an hour's time, still fonching for a battle, Gordon Rounding's Legion Hotel sped off toward its new objective.

"Well, that's that," Lloyd Harshman said dully. "I suppose we get our transport and herd these prisoners back to San José."

"Blackhawk One, this is Modoc Zero-zero." Mark Kelly's voice blared over the Cohort net.

"Blackhawk One, go," Harshman responded.

"Blackhawk One, you did an outstanding job and I'm putting you and your exec in for Legion Merit awards. Turn your prisoners over to Charlie Century and get some rest. Hot chow for everyone, if you've got it."

"What's the catch?" a combat-wise Harshman inquired.

"You have four hours to rest and resupply. Legion Golf is on the way to extract all Bravo Centuries. Enjoy your break and good luck."

Harshman and Hoover exchanged glances. "Awh, shit," Lt. Don Hoover voiced their thoughts. "Looks like the Bravos are about to get their feet wet."

A Costa Rican band played a typical Latin martial air while the graduating class of the first Legion Basic marched in review. Lt. Col. Chuck Taylor stood on the reviewing stand beside Gen. Porfirio Manual Kreutzer y Lopez, newly created Minister of Defense. The new cabinet member had a front on him like a pouter pigeon, resplendent in dark green dress uniform, white shirt, and black tie. Even with his high, peaked "flying saucer" hat, he didn't come to Chuck's shoulder. The trainees had spent only one day on dismounted drill, including ceremonies, and their lack of cadenced step bore witness to it.

No frills for these men. They had to become combat soldiers fast. All the same, Chuck felt great pride in their accomplishments. He had a prepared speech he would give later, but a large part of the day's scenario consisted of Taylor fielding questions and giving a lecture on the Legion's theory of modern warfare to newly commissioned officers of the Costa Rican Defense Force. When the ceremony ended, Chuck led the collection of neophytes to the officers' club and undertook that part of the task.

"Gentlemen, we strongly urge the employment of the Merlins, in all configurations, for good reason. Particularly because your needs can best be answered by their use. A single Merlin 400, fully armed, costs less than the basic airframe of a Huey. Further, the entire flyaway Merlin is less expensive than a replacement turbine for a Huey, not even counting the transmission. They'll run on anything except bunker fuel and urine. You don't have a lot of airfields here or a highly developed highway system. Yet, anywhere you can pack in a couple of drums of gasoline, some cases of oil and ammunition, you can service a Merlin. The VTOL characteristics make it a must."

"Also," Chuck went on, signaling the bartender for another beer, "a single Merlin 400 has the potential to kill up to six separate Armored Fighting Vehicles, exclusive of MBTs, which require heavier ordnance."

"We concede that the Legion has proven the validity of that point," Minister Kreutzer allowed. "Though, if it's all so easy, why, then, have you let the war bog down?"

"I'm sorry that I can't answer that," Chuck evaded. "I'm only a glorified schoolteacher, not a strategist. But I have absolute faith in General Watie, who is a superb strategist and masterful tactician."

Watie indeed had good reason to delay, Chuck reminded himself. First the Legion needed to train a competent defense force before the Red disinformation network inside the media demanded a Legion pullout. Secondly, he needed time for a direct invasion of Nicaragua to cut off Sandinista troops and equipment inside Costa Rica.

"Now," Lt. Col. Taylor went on, smiling at the knowledge his guests did not have, "this first class will become cadre to train ten times their number. Out of that group, those best qualified will be sent on to flight school to man Merlins when your government orders them." *Damn*, another invasion, Chuck fumed. And yet another he would have to miss.

* * *

Wisps of gray-edged black smoke rose from the last bastion of Sandinista resistance in Puerto Cabezas. For all practical purposes the city had fallen to the Miskito guerrillas. Seven men held on stubbornly for two days after the decisive attack that had taken the town. They had no hope, and knew it, for the Sandinistas didn't have enough shipping on the Caribbean side to bring in troops to retake Puerto Cabezas. The Miskitos treated the die-hards with indifference.

Occasionally they would break off from some other activity to fire a few shots into the thick-walled former tile factory, or lob a grenade through a shattered window. The "Spanish" Sandinistas would return fire or curse them and resume the waiting game. It was a dull sort of war, Cato Padilla considered, yet he could not stir his charges into finishing it in a final rush.

It was a dull sort of war for Arizona Jim Levin also. He had managed to repair Becky with fiberglass patches and ducting tape and flown her from the deck of his rescue ship to the Miskito camp in Honduras. Jay Solice greeted him warmly and put him to work.

"We've got eighteen Merlin Four Hundreds here and a dozen mercenary pilots to fly 'em. It'll be your job, Captain Levin, to familiarize these volunteers with the Merlin fighting system and Legion tactics."

"God, Colonel, you mean *I'm* going to be a *teacher*?" Arizona Jim gulped. He'd harbored high hopes of returning to combat in Costa Rica.

"You're what I've got," Jay stated simply.

Early the next morning, before even the macaws and parrots had begun their daily chatter, Arizona Jim fell out the mercs on the edge of the field. They responded well enough, he'd give them credit for that. And they didn't chatter like schoolboys. Like Jim, the rest wore flying jumpsuits, tan in color, with snaps, plugs, and gadget pockets built in. Unlike him, they wore neither insignia of rank nor a Legion shoulder patch. He wondered how they would respond to discipline.

To find out he called them to attention. Most snapped to

instantly. "Gentlemen, I'm Captain Levin. I'll be your
flight instructor for the purpose of familiarization with the
Merlin Four Hundred, gunnery, and Legion air tactics.
First off, how many of you have flying combat experience?" Might as well get that one out of the way up front.

"You two who raised your hands. Your names and where
did you see combat?"

"Pruitt, Robert, sir. In Chad, sir."

"Lockheart, Aaron, sir. In Chad, also, sir."

"You flew against Khaddafi's MiGs?" Arizona Jim
asked, impressed.

"Yes, sir," Bobby Pruitt responded. "They're not all
they're supposed to be, sir. Those sand crabs don't have a
natural feel for flying."

"Once a missile's locked on, it doesn't give a shit how
good the airplane driver is who fired it, Pruitt. Remember
that. I want you all to take a look at Becky over there. My
bird. See those patches? I was shot down over the Caribbean by a MiG-twenty-five. A Nicaraguan pilot. One nice
feature about the Merlin. It floats. Unless the bottom is
holed, it won't sink. Also, if you get into some real sticky
shit with a Four Hundred, it can take a greater impact
without sustaining damage than the pilot can survive. What
you have to remember is that if you are about to lose consciousness, go to autopilot. *Whether you are alive or not* it
will set you down easy. It's all automatic. Now then, you
two will be flight leaders. Alpha and Bravo Flights, under
my overall command. Each of you will be responsible for
five other birds."

For the next half hour, Arizona Jim went over the various stores assortments the M-400 could carry, the usual
groupings and their tactical employment. Then he put the
mercs through the paces, with hands-on talk-throughs of
the various firing controls. Noon chow call found them
hard at it.

"What pains my ass," Arizona Jim confided in the chow
line to M/Sgt. Ames, the ground crew chief, "is that we
don't have a Four Hundred Tee. I'm gonna sweat twelve
check rides this afternoon without dual controls to save my
ass. I'll be glad when they all solo."

"You take it too seriously, Captain," Ames assured him. "They're all a little blown over the reality of these birds, but I know they've read up on them and won't be inclined to overcontrol. The hard part will be getting them to talk to their aircraft."

"Yeah. And wait until target practice starts, day after tomorrow," Jim responded glumly.

"Our first live fire mission will be sort of a milk run," Arizona Jim informed the eager mercenaries four days later. "There's this little patrol boat that's been sneaking upriver and lobbing forty mike-mike shells into Puerto Cabezas. We're going to go kill that boat."

After a run-through of maps and some satellite photos of the river mouth around Puerto Cabezas, the pilots manned their planes. Arizona Jim listened to each bird report operational conditions. "Set ducts to hover mode," he commanded at last.

"Lift." Just giving the command filled Capt. Levin with excitement. The twelve craft gently rose three feet off the ground to match his position. "Merced tower, this is Savoy Zero zero," Jim informed the make-do control tower at the newly christened Campo Merced. "Ready for takeoff."

"Roger Savoy Zero zero. Altimeter is two-niner-niner, winds steady from zero-seven-zero, five knots. You are cleared for takeoff."

"Savoy Alpha One, Bravo One, you will execute a mass lift to form on me at five hundred Alpha-Golf-Lima after I clear the field. Over."

"Savoy Alpha One, roger that," Bobby Pruitt in Savoy Alpha One acknowledged. "Mass lift to five hundred AGL."

"Savoy Bravo One copies five hundred, that's a roger," Aaron Lockheart cheerfully responded.

When the speedy Merlin 400s all hovered at five hundred feet above ground level, Arizona Jim gave the command to move out. "Savoy flight, fly nap-of-the-earth to avoid exposure, and maintain three-seven-five knots until target is in sight. Acknowledge."

Half a minute went by while the individual pilots informed their flight leaders. "Savoy Leader, this is Savoy Bravo One, all copy NOTE, at three-seven-five knots."

"Savoy Leader, this is Savoy Alpha One, all copy as given."

Their run to Puerto Cabezas, which had taken a week to accomplish on the ground, took only minutes. "Savoy Flight, I have Puerto Cabezas in sight," Arizona Jim announced. He changed frequencies and keyed his mike. "Modoc Shotgun Two, this is Savoy Zero zero. Is your visitor in sight? Over."

"Savoy Zero zero, this is Shotgun Two. Roger that. He's lobbin' 'em in right regular. We're all under cover. Over."

"Can you vector me, over?"

"Savoy Zero zero, make a straight in across town on zero-two-five and you can catch him at the big bend." A shell exploded in the background.

"That's a roger, Modoc Shotgun Two," Arizona Jim responded. "Savoy Alpha and Bravo, form two lines on me, maintain fifteen-second intervals, then turn to heading zero-two-five. Bring up your stores, arm weapons. We'll go in with three-point-fives first. Copy, over."

Acknowledgments came quickly. These guys were eager, Arizona Jim credited them. They whipped in over town in stair-stepped formation, line astern. Arizona Jim saw the big bend of the river grow in his HUD stadia and picked out the little riverboat a few seconds before the crew saw the Merlins. White foam churned at the stern of the gunboat as it attempted to make a run for it. With deft touches of his controls, Jim kept the vessel lined up.

"Firing," he announced over the squadron net.

A pair of 3.5-inch rockets detached from their pods, ignited and sped toward the desperate craft. Arizona Jim nosed up and pulled out of the pattern as Bobby Pruitt, leading Savoy Alpha, loosed his first two missiles. The river flashed past under the Merlin's gracefully contoured lift body and the jungle rose toward the nimble craft. Capt. Jim Levin continued to climb, confident the merc pilots behind would do the same. At three thousand, he leveled

out and began a wide turn. In half a minute he could see
the result of their first attack run.

Five of the birds in Savoy Alpha had completed their
approach. A monumental column of smoke, flame, and
water rose from the surface of the river, where the gunboat
had been. Bits of debris, from tiny to huge, pocked the
water with white splashes. Instantly, Arizona Jim keyed his
mike.

"Enough! Enough, already. Break off. There's nothing
left to shoot."

Radio procedure be damned, Jim thought. Why waste
ammunition. Twenty seconds more over the target area
proved how wrong his statement had been. A bright flash
of a missile detonating in the aft fan array of a Savoy
Bravo craft blasted all the pilots out of their euphoric overconfidence. Before the injured Merlin reported trouble,
Arizona Jim spotted the source.

"That sure's hell wasn't in the scenario," Capt. Levin
said aloud as he stared disbelievingly at the 300 mph Soviet Hokum helio. It bore in on the small formation, ready-
ing to fire at another surprised craft. Jim opened the
squadron net.

"Savoy Squadron, this is Savoy One. Bandit at one
o'clock, level. Verify a Hokum attack helicopter. Let's
double gang him. Savoy Bravo take him low and first,
Savoy Alpha go in high and second. Execute."

"Savoy One, this is Savoy Bravo Four. My tail's afire
and I'm ditching in the river. This *is* a Mayday, out."

Captain Antonio Curzon of the Cuban air force had
flown his Hokum out of the embattled Sandinista base at
Yacaltara to protect the precious craft from possible cap-
ture. Fully armed, he brought it north in time to witness the
attack on the riverboat. The element of surprise rested with
him. He took immediate advantage of it. His first missile
blasted one of the Merlins' engines out of existence, with
another askew on its mounts and flames whipping in the
wash of the remaining fans. Quickly he readied another.

"Ramón, take manual control of your weapon. Start cutting up those monstrosities," he commanded on the intercom.

A moment later the four barrels of a 23mm cannon began to rotate and spit explosive shells at another of the darting Merlins. Capt. Curzon suppressed a triumphant grin as he released another missile. A moment later a bright flash bloomed, actinic white, in a flurry of chaff. The target skidded to a stop and hurtled directly upward. Without pause it jinked to the right and the simpleminded missile detonated by proximity fuse a hundred feet from the decoy.

"How can that be?" Capt. Curzon asked his copilot.

"If I hadn't seen it, I'd never believe it," Senior Lieutenant Villalobos responded. "Not even the Yanqui Air Force has something like that."

Lights went wild on the combat analyzer. Threats seemed to bloom above them from all points of the compass. Amber lights turned to red as new challenges came from below, yet the screen showed no enemy aircraft, only missiles. Curzon's hands on the collective and cyclic controls flooded with moisture. Where had they come from? The most pressing threat repeated on the screen in front of him.

Instinctively Capt. Curzon whipped the helicopter sideways. A small, stubby 3.5 rocket flashed past the windscreen, within inches of the outer arc of the twin rotor blades. It disappeared below, much to the pilot's relief. Another menace appeared and he fired three decoy flares. Too late he realized that these diminutive missiles were neither radar nor IR guided.

"*Se me pararon los pelos este!*" Capt. Antonio Curzon exclaimed in a shaken tone when the first missile missed them.

It would scare the daylights out of anyone, he thought, to see a missile successfully pass through the minute spaces of their counterrotating main rotors. The Soviet 23mm continued to hammer. Luckily, his copilot had not seen the close call. Curzon twisted the Hokum to locate another likely target.

In his overwhelming relief at the narrow passage of death, Capt. Antonio Curzon forgot about the other incoming missiles. A fraction of a second after he saw a Merlin fire two 3.5 rockets his way, another, from below and behind, caught up to him and the Hokum became a yellow-white fireball. Shreds and lumps of metal and men twisted in the shockwave that followed the violent explosion.

CHAPTER
18

Raucous parrots, finches, macaws, and other feathered creatures of the jungle nearly drowned out human speech. Capt. Jim Levin reported directly to Lt. Col. Jay Solice immediately after debriefing, as ordered. He saluted smartly and waited for the axe to fall. Four aircraft shot up, one completely out of action; having put the fire out it had been towed ashore by Miskitos. Two pilots wounded, one seriously. *Of course* the grisly blade would eventually drop.

"Captain Levin, it was not the purpose of this 'milk run' mission to lose aircraft or get pilots shot up," Lt. Col. Solice grated out.

"I'm aware of that, Colonel," Arizona Jim said contritely.

"All the same," Jay pressed on, allowing a tiny hint of a grin to appear. "Your makeshift squadron accounted for that pesky gunboat and got a bonus of a Hokum chopper. In a word, it's a job well done. Now then, the purpose of this conference, and that of having my own independent command of Merlins, is what is to be done once General Watie runs out of stall."

"Sir?" Jim questioned.

"Surely you realize, Captain, that General Watie can

bullshit only so long, keep the conflict inside Costa Rican territory only so long, and flimflam Congress only so long. Eventually the Kremlin is going to feel directly threatened by our presence in Central America. When they do, all those whining whelps in Congress are going to wag their tails and rush to do their Master's bidding. They can't actually force us out. But it's only three months until the election. They can make things so rough for the President and his hopes for the future of the Legion that a withdrawal becomes mandatory."

Jay paused and paced the floor a moment. He stopped by a window and gazed out at the Miskito refugee village that sprawled around their hill. A heavy sigh escaped him. "If we have not finished our task here when that happens, I'll resign from the Legion rather than desert the Miskitos. I grew up on an Apache reservation in Arizona. You've seen them, I'm sure. Christ, the squalor was no worse than what these people endured before we came. The point is, no one, *not one single human being*, should be compelled to live like that. Damnit, I'm an Indian, so are they." He ceased abruptly.

"I suppose that's an ethereal concept that's hard to convey to non-Indians," Jay apologized.

Jim Levin thought of the defenders of Massada, of those who died in the burning ghettos of medieval Europe, and fought for an answer. It came hard around the lump in his throat. "No. It's not so difficult as you'd think. I've only been here a short while. But . . . they get to grow on you. It's the kids . . . the old people . . . hooo-boy! You ain't gonna believe this. I even felt sorry for the way the Palestinians were treated by Israel. Nobody has a right to treat people in such a shitty way. If you stay, I'll stay. D'you think General Watie'll support us?"

In three swift strides, Jay crossed the room and wrung Jim's hand. "You bet he will," he said through a grin. "It would leave a Legion presence in Central America. Never mind it would be a tenuous connection, we'd be the vanguard of their return. And you can bet that if it isn't finished now, the Legion will have to come back some time."

"Then we're together in this?" Arizona Jim asked, chest swelling.

"You bet we are. Do or die," Lt. Col. Solice assured him.

Sniffing the salty tang of the sparkling Pacific, Chris Anderson, First Sergeant of Bravo, Second, worked at the cud in his cheek and spat out a stream of brown tobacco juice. He took care to see it went to leeward. "I never thought a jungle could smell sweet and inviting," he offered to a fellow noncom.

They stood near the bow of the renovated and recommissioned though still decrepit LST LSS *Martin Jacobs*. The Bravos stood well out to sea. After a month of intensive landing practice prior to heading for Costa Rica, both the green Legion crews and the Bravos could be rated as fairly good at amphibious operations. Competence did little to soften the impact on these foot soldiers at being back on the water again.

"I know what you mean," Sgt. Brian Connor agreed. "We ain't looking at the easiest job the Legion's ever done."

"You got that right. Hey, look over there. We got company," Chris announced.

Another LST steamed under full power to join up with those running in tandem toward Puntarenas. Around them the Legion Task Force provided an over-the-horizon security screen. The large white bone in the teeth of the newcomer subsided as she pulled into formation.

"I wonder if the guys on that one like this any better than us?" Connor asked idly.

Lt. Col. Bob Fuller stood on the flying bridge of the LST *Frank Minor*, and gazed at the two sister ships they approached. The large, heavy, light-gathering naval glasses he used brought detail into sharp clarity. He even saw the stream of tobacco juice one Legionnaire spat over the side of the LST slightly in the lead.

"I don't know if we're gonna do any good where we're headin'," he remarked to a young lieutenant at his side.

"But I know one thing. It's going to be a bitch to get all these tanks off without incident. We've only had one platoon that trained at it before the operation. If the Sandinistas have their shit together on that beach, we could lose a lot of men and equipment."

"You'd rather be back in the jungle, crossing those mountains, sir?" the junior officer inquired.

"I'd rather be back with my old lady, on Cat Cay, barbecuing some steaks and drinking beer," Fuller stated sincerely. "Don't get me wrong. I like what I'm doing. In fact, I *love* a good fight. But we could have used a couple of more months in training. Thing like this, these people should be able to do in their sleep."

From the pilot-house door the captain of the *Frank Minor* called to Fuller. "Train your glasses to port, Colonel Fuller. You'll get a good view of the *Scipio*. She'll be coming over the horizon any minute now. They're cleared for sunset landing exercises. Taking aboard a squadron of Merlins."

"Thanks, Captain," Bob responded. He hefted the heavy glasses and placed them on another pintle mount. Swiveling left and right, he soon located the high island of the *Scipio*, floating unrealistically above the demarcation line of sky and water.

While he watched, entranced by the quirks of light and movement, the squadron of Merlins flocked in to join the naval Harriers on the *Scipio*. Swinging and swaying, tilting as though on an invisible axis, the little birds put on a spectacular aerial ballet. Two at a time they would fall from the formation, match velocity and hover over the flight deck a moment, then drop softly to their landing. Played against the spectacular backdrop of the setting sun, the mundane maneuvers took on the aspects of a surreal picture. Like the daubs, slashes, and strokes of a South Seas artist's palate on virgin canvas, the scarlet, gold, and magenta bars of light that lay on the gently heaving breast of the Pacific framed a painting of tranquility that tugged at the heart.

His coronary pangs heightened and a sharp gasp of awed appreciation escaped Lt. Col. Bob Fuller when nature

gifted him with that most fleeting and precious of sights. In
that spellbound moment when the great orange globe
drowned in the ocean, Bob saw a vivid flash of purest
emerald green.

Strapped into a crash couch, in a semireclining position
against the bulkhead of a 56-foot Hecate fast patrol boat,
Sergeant Michael Anthony Hoxsey watched in horrified
fascination as the huge cargo door beyond the stern ground
open. *Holy oh, Lord fuck a wild man*, he thought frantically. He thoroughly believed that anyone who jumped out
of perfectly good airplanes was a fucking idiot. Now here
he was, about to be *yanked* out of one, boat and all. A
sudden bump told him the C-5 transport had crossed the
shore of Lake Nicaragua and he gripped the nylon ripcord
tighter in a sweaty palm.

"Keep braced . . . watch the red light," Mike shouted
over the engine roar to his crew. Following the careful instructions, he made the double check at the last moment to
be sure.

Sweating profusely, hating being in this place, Mike
looked at his watch. Right on schedule: 2330 hours. Suddenly a green light came on beside the red one. Mike acti-
vated the release lever to free his boat, then yanked the
ripcord. Following the pilot chute, green nylon blotted out
the stars and the suspension lines rapidly lost their slack. A
moment later, the big patrol boat was jerked rudely from its
second-tier position in the belly of the gigantic bird. Mike's
stomach began to rebel as the clamshell doors flashed past.

Falling faster than any express elevator, the Kevlar boat
plummeted toward earth. A line attached to the bow triggered the 'chute of the boat on the lower tier. The second
boat became airborne, as another cargo 'chute deployed
above Mike and the giddy descent arrested abruptly. An
instant later the 56-foot boat crashed into the water with a
terrific impact that would have shattered a lesser craft.
Stunned, Mike fumbled at the quick release box on his
harness. Tasting blood from a nipped lip, he stumbled aft
to haul the 'chute aboard, while his AA gunner set up the

triple-tube Javelin launcher and the radarman went groaning to raise his mast.

Two minutes after splashdown, the Hecate's big Merlin diesels roared to life and she began to search for a fight. In the area close inboard, Mike scanned nineteen other patrol boats in various states of readiness. Satisfied at his own condition and that of the tiny fleet, he keyed his squad net helmet mike.

"This is Fido, operational and ready for orders."

Sargento Primero Juan Carlos Sepeda picked up his bullhorn and challenged the black shape that loomed monstrous in the starlit waters of the little bay of San Juan. First Sergeant Sepeda did not like his assignment to the coastal patrol units of the Ejercitos Poblaras Sandinistas. The motion of boats made him queasy, his appetite suffered, his skin developed a salty rash. Yet he was here in San Juan del Sur to serve the state. He would serve it as directed. It was night duty like this that particularly discouraged him. The unknown vessel had not responded, he noted, with a testy "tisk" of tongue on palate. With a sigh of resignation he lifted the loud hailer to his lips again.

"Unidentified vessel, show a light. What is your business here? Contact Port Authority on one-three-seven megahertz and identify yourself. Unidentified vessel, show a light or you will be fired upon."

From the railing of the mystery ship came a dim flash. A moment later the rugged outline of the LST's superstructure was lighted by the glaring, pale violet light of an Eryx missile's main propulsion motor. At Mach 5, the missile had covered three-quarters of the distance before Juan Sepeda realized that his small power launch had been fired upon. Juan Carlos Sepeda's world suddenly turned bright white and the deck slammed so violently against his feet that it shattered his spine and he never noticed the transition to Marxist limbo. Echoes of the explosion rolled across the water.

At the EPS coastal patrol garrison of San Juan del Sur, Juan Carlos's demise created quite a stir. The rumble of the blast still reached them as half-dressed men poured from the barracks into direct fire from a destroyer's five-inch thirty-eights. Inexplicably, deadly little aircraft fell from the sky to deliver cargoes of hot steel and high explosive on their tender young bodies. As though sickened by all the excitement she had initiated, the LST made her way cautiously to a wide, sandy beach and opened her vast maw. Wrapped in cloying diesel fumes, she vomited up Legion armor all over Playa Bonita.

While his Commando Stingray disgorged from the *Martin Jacobs*, Lt. Col. Bob Fuller checked his watch: 0006. That put them five minutes behind schedule. "Keep it moving," he shouted, uncaring that his voice could not be heard over the rumble and roar of the powerful tank engines.

By radio, Lt. Col. Fuller began to bring order out of the chaotic beach scene. Columns were formed up and the first elements started off for San Jorge Rivas, to cut the Pan American Highway there and take the Sandinista supply dumps. He went over the battle plan with his subordinate commanders as he gave orders.

"Once at San Jorge, you're to leave a blocking force while the rest of the Century heads for Cardenas. That'll give us command of the western and southern shore of Lake Nicaragua and secure the Costa Rican border. All platoon leaders take note. It is imperative that we have this done before dawn. The Sandinista air force is down to flying daylight missions only. With most of their airborne search and ground radar installations out, they're damned near confined to Visual Flight Rules operation," Fuller explained lightly. "Even so, with the sun comes the enemy air."

CHAPTER
19

Although casting frequent, apprehensive glances skyward, the citizens of San José, Costa Rica, went about their morning routine as usual. Some walked close to the buildings, while vehicular traffic had dwindled somewhat. Outside of these few indicators, one could not tell that this was the capital city of a nation at war, one that enemy aircraft could easily reach and might bombard. The leading daily newspapers, *La Nación, La República,* and *La Prensa Libre*, along with television and radio news, had informed the people that the American Foreign Legion had achieved air superiority and there would be no more raids. The Legion received fulsome praise for this accomplishment. At the urging of the President, the Legislative Assembly had voted to strike a Medal of Valor, to be given to all Legion pilots who participated in freeing the nation from the danger of Nicaraguan air attack. Major Mick Orenda brought news of that, along with other, pressing information to Gen. Norman Watie over breakfast coffee.

"Not surprisingly," Mick observed, "there's been little opposition. In light of the Nicaraguan invasion, the Friends of Sandino are keeping their mouths shut. I've saved the best news for last. Operation Anvil is in place. We should have tactical control of the lake within five hours."

"That's pushing it a little, isn't it?" Watie inquired, peering over the magnifying half-glasses he wore to read a copy of the *Tico Times*, the English-language San José newspaper. Vanity, he admitted, wouldn't let him get examined for regular spectacles and the idea of contacts seemed somehow ghoulish.

"Not really. For all practical purposes we have de facto control of the lake now. The Harley boats are sweeping the lake of shipping. In fact, they've captured an entire armored division loaded on barges. The prisoners and equipment will have to be taken out by LST. With adequate air cover we can have full control by this time tomorrow morning."

"That *is* good news. Alright, now's the time to put on the squeeze. I want the Harleys, the fifty-sixes and sixty-fours, to carry Merlins in close enough for strikes against military targets around all the major cities in Nicaragua. See to it, Mick."

Mark McDade looked over the sharp-edged rubble on the volcanic island of Isla de Ometepa. The forbidding landscape gave him a feeling of standing on the moon. Fortunately, the Merlins had little trouble landing there. Building a proper airstrip would be a nightmare. His reflections ended when Major Dick House approached.

"I don't know how people live here, but they do," Dick observed. The buckskin hunting shirt he wore contrasted wildly with his cammo trousers. His sandy brown hair looked darker around the edges where the humidity had induced heavy perspiration. "And we've got a delegation of locals who want to help us. I need another Spanish speaker there and you're it, Mark. The natives have, ah, expressed considerable gratitude for our, ah, 'liberation.' And I gather what they want now is to identify the communists among their number and purge the island of Sandinistas."

"My, it's amazing what a little backbone will do for people. Even when it's someone else's," Mark remarked cynically.

Maj. House frowned. "Don't let them catch the least hint

that you consider them anything less than die-hard patriots.
We've got it made here. Our supplies are being ferried in
by chopper on a regular basis, the small-boat people
beached one of the captured fuel barges and we've even
got willing and eager native labor to help set up our base."

"Ah, yes, Shangri-la in the midst of Lake Nicaragua,"
Mark quipped. "Seriously, Dick, I'm sure you're right.
I've had the feeling since we landed that we've got our part
of this war by the balls. Let's go interrogate our willing
snitches."

By evening, the light-weight pavilions had all been
erected. The mess hall, barracks, maintenance shops, and a
beer hall. With Sandinista air grown sparse, even within
Nicaragua, the men had time to relax before launching the
newly ordered strikes on military targets at dawn. Capt.
Mark McDade took his leisure to listen to an English-
language news broadcast.

"Reports of terrifying air raids come from Managua tonight. Although parts of the city are supposed to be in
flame, the Sandinista government of Daniel Ortega continues bravely to resist the pirates of the American Foreign
Legion," a dry, British-accented voice informed Mark.
"Without provocation, the Legion has struck deep into the
heart of Nicaragua, in violation of international law. It
gives cause to wonder where it will all end. Will Hunter's
Liberty Corps invade Washington, D.C.? Will there be
tanks in Foggy Bottom? Although the Legion is the inven-
tion of Lame Duck President Dalton Hunter, the chief executive seems unable, or unwilling, to curb their excesses.
At the United Nations today, a resolution was introduced to
send a peacekeeping force to Nicaragua to contain the invasion before it has a chance to spread. Bogged down in
debate, it has not moved off the floor of the General Assembly to the Security Council. Meanwhile, President
Fidel Castro has offered to send troops to stop the fascistic
Liberty Corps. It is believed that Daniel Ortega will accept
this offer of aid within the next twenty-four hours. We will
be back with more hemispheric happenings following these
important messages."

"You son of a b——..." Mark blurted, his curse cut off by the arrival of his first sergeant.

"New orders, sir."

"What now?" Mark growled. "Are we being pulled out to please the suck-asses in Congress?"

"No, sir. Quite the contrary," Leicestershire-born John Edson said through a grin. "We're to stage a rocket attack on the rail yards in Managua at oh-six-hundred hours."

"All riiiight!" Mark shouted like a kid when the home team belted in a four-bagger home run.

"Comrade Arkady Petrovich Gulyakin, you have served the Rodina and the Party well for many years. The time has come to receive recognition for this," the General Secretary intoned in solemn cadences.

Red banners flew over Red Square; bunting along the walls of the Kremlin wafted gently in a light breeze. Uniformed ranks of KGB, the Army, and the entire Politburo filled Peter's Square inside. They had all come to honor Arkady Gulyakin.

"Your elevation to the rank of *Podpolkovnik* has already been confirmed. Now you are to assume a new and prestigious position as Chief Instructor at the Cham-Beykor espionage and terrorist school."

"But, my successful program to eliminate the American Foreign Legion," Arkady blurted out, committing the terrible sin of interrupting the head of the Party. "I must be free to carry it to a conclusion."

"Others will follow in your brilliant footsteps, Comrade," the General Secretary informed him. "For you there is a whole new world of experience, far from the mundane activities of a field agent. Rejoice that the Party knows your work and is properly grateful for it."

"But, I ... but I ..."

Arkady Gulyakin awakened in his bed in a New York luxury hotel, chilled by icy perspiration. *"Borgemoi*, oh my God," he exclaimed out loud.

It had seemed so real. He had really been inside the Kremlin. To have triumphed and to have failed all in one. To be rewarded and "kicked upstairs" for the incompetence of being caught. Yet, the exchange had not as yet been negotiated. He waited, under FBI guard, in the Hotel Astor in Manhattan, well fed, with all the liquor he wanted, even women when needed. A VIP, though a prisoner as well. What would it really be like, he wondered, when he returned to Moscow?

The Legion staff huddled around their Commander's TV set in his San José quarters. The cause for this unusual scene was a satellite broadcast of commentary on the presidential election campaign. Although showing his age, John Chancellor retained all the fire and vigor of his long career. His face predicted doom and his words rang with righteous indignation.

"Election years have always been fertile ground for sprouting unusal events. Most notable has to be this one. Events in Nicaragua and Costa Rica spell disaster for the North-Hunter ticket. Their open support for the crazed aggressors of the Liberty Corps, who have invaded the sovereign territory of Nicaragua without even a formal declaration of war, has turned popular opinion against Lieutenant Colonel North and the President. Although he was vindicated in the Iran-Contra scandal, the shadow of that blight still lays across Oliver North. The President has had a successful, but rocky, road these past seven years. Now comes the Legion's unwarranted adventurism to haunt them. Reliable sources close to the National Committee have revealed to NBC News that a number of party leaders have seriously considered withdrawing official support for their candidacy. This, of course, would create turmoil for the upcoming election.

"It's never easy, being a lame duck president, and it's not easy to admit a mistake of catastrophic proportions. President Hunter finds himself in both of these positions right now. Over the weeks that the Legion has pushed its aggression in Central America, some on Capitol Hill have asked that the President resign. Others in the Halls of Congress have demanded an impeachment. The solution is simple. With a stroke of a pen, President Hunter can dissolve the connection between the United States and the

Legion. All he need do then is join the United Nations in
supporting a peacekeeping force to apprehend these international criminals and bring an end to the threat to stability
in Central America. It just might save him the next election. From this removed and unbiased position the alterna-
tive, it seems, is political suicide. This is John Chancellor
and that's my opinion for tonight."

"Somebody ought to feed *him* a can of Drano," Maj.
Danvors, the Deputy G-4, growled.

"He's protected by the right of free speech," Mick Orenda pointed out, not at all happy about it.

"'Protected' and 'free' only so long as you agree with
those bastards," Danvors snapped in his own defense.

"Gentlemen, we have to put politics aside. We have
more battles to win. It's still better than two months to the
election. If we pull this off, Ollie and Dalton can parade
unprotected down the streets of Boston and the Secret Service won't have to worry."

"Don't be too sure," Lt. Col. Pat Andrews's voice of
doom and gloom invaded the cheerful prediction.

Lying down in ditches and getting shot at was not the
purpose for which Pepe Lazar had joined the EPS. Swag-
gering through the streets of Managua in uniform, catching
the eyes of all the girls, now *that* was what being a soldier
was all about. Pepe didn't mind destroying a few back-
water villages and killing the occupants to provide "evidence" for the world press of the atrocities of the
anti-Sandinista guerrillas. After all, bean farmers didn't
shoot back. And he looked forward to exporting their glori-
ous revolution to other countries in Central America. Soon
they would move on that monster, Mexico. The Red ban-
ner would fly from the Rio Bravo del Norte to the Colom-
bian border. Then the corrupt, imperialist Estados Unidos
would fall apart from internal rot and the threat of invasion.

Power to the people! Pepe loved to march in parades.
What he didn't love were mortars. The musical flutter of
incoming 81mm bombs turned his heart to ice and his
bowels to water. A wet warmth spread from his crotch as

his bladder let go. The ground began to rock and roll with the rippling detonations of mortar rounds. Dust choked him, his eyes teared from it. Gouts of turf flew skyward. A thin, high sound, gaining in volume and substance, came from beyond the clearing.

"Yeeeeee-aaaaaaah-hoooooo!"

¡*Por dios!* Here they came. The American Foreign Legion. Those madmen with the huge, horrible bayonets. *"Mamacita, ayudame, por favor."*

"This one was callin' for his Momma," a burly Legion corporal remarked as he toed the corpse of Pepe Lazar with his boot.

"Funny what a feller thinks of in combat," his sergeant remarked. "I was wishin' for my Maw, too. Then we rolled 'em up so easy. I felt kinda foolish. Hope they're together now."

"Jeez, Serge, I never knew you were so sentimental."

"Bullshit!" the sergeant snapped. "Keep a sharp eye, Corporal. We've got a thousand prisoners to deal with."

Melted into a Daliesque cyclorama, the walls of high-rise buildings streaked past Mark McDade's Merlin as he screamed through the streets of Managua, Nicaragua, on another low-level attack at four hundred miles per hour. Ahead of him a platoon of tanks escorted firefighting equipment toward the blazing railroad yards. He placed the lead T-72 in the stadia of his HUD and fired a missile.

Smoke and fragments of steel flew higher than his own trajectory. Mark pulled up slightly and sought new targets. The Legion net had recently broadcast that the EPS Army of the South had surrendered at Villa Canaste, Costa Rica. That removed the danger within their sponsor country. He also sensed, in not receiving an order to break off the attack, that Gen. Watie had something else up his sleeve. Mark caught sight of a greater threat to his Merlins than the tanks.

Two Soviet ZSU-23-4, quad-barreled, track-mounted antiaircraft units squirted in and out of hiding, twisting through the streets and seeking shots at the zipping little craft. Mark made a short 30mm run and a game of cat-and-mouse developed.

Two ZSU-23-4s clearly made the game a deadly one. For the Merlins they were the most fearsome weapon in the Soviet arsenal. The automatic cannon responded quite rapidly to eyeball aiming and manual controls. Mark had previously lost a forward engine to one, and was understandably a bit nervous. He reduced speed, turned a corner, and keyed a burst at one of the infernal devices. Below, people in the street cheered for the little Legion bird. Mark felt less alone, but no less uncomfortable. He cut right, then right again.

Dropping to ground level, Mark reversed his route and sped along a parallel side street to where he'd last seen the ZSUs. A quick turn and he caught them from behind. He hit the arm switch for a Javelin unit and released the missile.

The Javelin rammed into the engine compartment of the ZSU and turned it into a huge fireball. Instantly Mark jerked his bird into a spiraling climb to escape the other ZSU's murderous fire. He cut around a five-story building, then ascended, to peek over the roof. He found the second Soviet AA unit burst into flame. A quick check showed no other Merlin close-by. The crew of the ZSU began to bail out.

Then a kid with a Molotov cocktail ran out of an alley and splashed the escaping Sandinista soldiers with flaming gasoline. At once people ran into the street and waved to Mark. Several raised their arms, two fingers separated in the V-sign for victory. Grinning, Mark turned toward a badly shot-up Sandinista garrison near the shore of Lake Managua. To his surprise, when he flashed over the rows of barracks, a full-fledged battle was in progress, apparently between the garrison and Sandinista Militia units. Not knowing which side to take, Mark decided to leave well enough alone. With a sigh of relief, he headed for home.

CHAPTER
20

Not everyone in Nicaragua celebrated the collapse of the Sandinista government. Many citizens, those who had received largesses of land or positions of power within the Departments or city governments, saw only ruin and despair in the upheaval. To them, the face of Daniel Ortega on television, twisted in expressions of anguish and bitterness, to match his impassioned words, said it all.

"My nation has been ravaged by a huge force of international pirates. As I speak to you," Ortega bleated from the safety of the Government Palace in Havana, "the people of Nicaragua lie prostrate under the jackboots of the American Foreign Legion which press upon their throats. I cry out to the freedom-loving peoples of the world to avenge this heinous crime."

Major Mick Orenda's left eyebrow raised to an alarming height at this and he studied the lightweight, treebark-patterned issue boot on his foot. "Is that guy for real?" he asked, then snorted with derision as the scene shifted to the New York studio.

Treavor Wellington, the new pundit of commentary at ABC News, had preheated his vocal chords so that his voice rang with the full timbre of his indignation. "It is heartening to see that even in his exile Daniel Ortega has the courage to challenge the oppressors of Nicaragua. The war has been a short one, barely a month in duration, yet already the Liberty Corps is making the weight of its tyranny felt from Managua to Lake Nicaragua. Experts in the field of political science and government have long agreed that the United States Constitution is outmoded, not relevant to the conditions of the twentieth, let alone the twenty-first, century. Now the Legion adds its own abuses by forcing an antiquated version of this document on the Chamber of Deputies it has raised up in the wake of the Sandinista collapse.

"Most disturbing to the democratic peoples of the world are the limits placed on the franchise under this spurious form of the Constitution. Only the literate may vote in the upcoming elections, the Legion has decreed. Worse, they have imposed a poll tax. Worst of all, the new government of this, ah, Republic of Nicaragua has been restricted to excise taxes, while the various Departments can institute only property taxes." Wellington shook his leonine mane of silvery hair and leaned a confidential elbow on the desk. "It doesn't take an economist to know that with no better funding than this a sovereign state cannot exist in the modern world. From where would they obtain the funding to support the bureaucracy? How would the civil service be paid? And what about maintaining a military force? The smirking statement of the outlaw Legion's commandant, General Watie that, and I quote, 'Costa Rica did quite well fifty years without an army,' is no answer at all. So while we grieve for Nicaragua's loss of liber——."

"Do newscasters, and commentators in particular, live on and observe the same planet as the rest of us?" Gen. Watie wondered aloud as he snapped off the set. He turned about to face the assembled staff. In the distance, beyond the spacious accommodations in Managua's Ministry of Interior building, vehicles rumbled in a steady stream. Legion military government units were being dispatched with non-Sandinista Militia to provide protection of property in outlying communities.

"Our first order of business is the bad news. When I spoke with the President, he informed me that Arkady Gulyakin has been exchanged for the American students arrested in Moscow two months ago. For the time being, there's nothing we can do. But, I'm not going to mark 'Closed' on his file as yet. Now, on to better things. Despite what the prophets of doom on the tube have to say, orders are being cut for Col. Chuck Taylor. You're to move the training camp to the vicinity of Cardenas, Nicaragua, on the border of Costa Rica, Chuck. There you will train troops for both countries, along with recruit Centuries of the Legion. That will continue until you have established a competent, professional officer corps for both of our hosts."

"Even though I suspect the reason, why train our own people here?" Chuck Taylor inquired.

"The Legion has outgrown Corsair Cay, Chuck. By the time you've completed your assignment here, I'll have drained the brains of the staff to find and establish a suitable location for future training. Commodore McDade will conduct naval training on the old facility at the Cay. Walt." Gen. Watie turned to his military government expert. "You'll stay on in Managua. The Nicaraguans are good people. They deserve a better way of life than Ortega and his Red scum gave them. As the Legion representative to the Chamber of Deputies, I'll trust that you see they get that chance. You'll have your office and quarters in the old Cuban Embassy building and I imagine you'll want to send for Maria to join you."

"That's fine with me. What will I have to work with?"

"I'll leave you the Century of your choice, to aid in the transition period to elected civil government. Moving right along, there's a young lieutenant, Cato Padilla, who has developed remarkable rapport with the Miskito Indians. I want G-One to cut orders for him to remain in the new autonomous Department of Mosquitia, with the task of introducing the Miskitos to the twenty-first century. That'll mean primary and secondary schooling, some organization of their economy, and, especially, minimal government."

"Just a suggestion, General," Lt. Col. Jay Solice injected. "Wouldn't it be advisable to have Padilla address the terrible race prejudice between the so-called 'Spanish' and the Indians?"

"Of course it would, Jay," Watie returned. "Yet the only tool that Padilla will have is equality before the law. Whether Indian, Negro, or Spanish, the people of Nicaragua are the same as anyone else. Given the insurance, enforced when necessary, that the government will respect and preserve the law and the rights of citizens with equal zeal, they'll find common grounds on which to build. Given that, false prejudice will die a natural, if slow, death. Also tell your prize lieutenant that he is to try to interest the Miskitos in consumer goods."

Lt. Col. Solice laughed lightly. "That's already accomplished. They all want Merlins."

"Andy," Watie went on, addressing Lt. Col. Andrews. "I want you to remain in Costa Rica with another Century and a staff of your choice until native troops are trained up and can be officered by Legionnaires. That's all at this time. Gentlemen," the general concluded, his voice warm with camaraderie. "This is our last staff conference in Nicaragua. The *Patches* and the *Meteor* are already loaded at San Juan del Sur. A motorcade is waiting for myself and the departing staff members. It's been a good campaign, but costly. I'll see you all again, at the Cay, with a flock of promotions, soon as you're released from here and the Tee-Oh can be altered accordingly. Now, I have to go play the buffoon and address the troops. Dismissed."

Captain Jim Levin rejoined his squadron three days after the last fanatic Sandinistas capitulated. His Merlin hummed beautifully, despite the numerous patches from enemy fire that adorned the skin. He flashed in over Managua at a sedate three hundred miles per hour, contemplating the future.

The Indians were going to be looked out for, helped and made secure in their own domain. One problem down. He'd be going back to the Cay. Taken together, life seemed rather sweet. Too bad he'd missed the fighting, but there'd be another time. What he ought to do is think about the squadron. He also might give some consideration to that lieutenant with the lovely body. Pretty nurses were a weakness he liked to indulge. Yes, he had a lot of catching up to do.

They stood at parade rest in silent, respectful ranks. The crested combat helmets had been replaced by gold berets. When Gen. Norman Stand Watie stepped out through the tall glass doors, the stentorian voice of Alden "Pops" Henderson bellowed: "At—ten-tion!" The Legion Sergeant Major then turned and saluted Gen. Watie. "Sir, the men . . . they'd like to hear a word from you, sir."

Although prepared for it, Watie produced a pained expression. "Very well, Sergeant Major. What is it I'm supposed to say?"

Pops, the oldest man in the Legion, produced a lopsided grin. "You know, sir, about how they did, what we accomplished. That, ah, sort of thing."

"As you will, Sergeant Major. At ease. The Legion fought like tigers," Gen. Watie began, raising his voice to a roar. "You all did well. The proof of it is that you're still here to listen to this. We lost seven hundred men, with a shade over a thousand wounded. The amount and cost of the equipment we lost staggers the imagination. But, by God, we won! In terms of captured equipment, we'll come out of this with a bit of a profit. Now I know that you didn't come here to listen to an accountant spout off. You did your duty and you came through it. The Legion will live on. Some thirty years ago, before a lot of you were born, a musical group performed a song that had a line in it to the effect that today is the first day of the rest of your life. I think it only proper that we carry that thought in our hearts as we make ready to return to Corsair Cay. To missing comrades!"

"To missing comrades," the assembled troops echoed resoundingly.

"Thank you all for your best efforts. You're still some of the meanest sons of bitches on the face of this earth . . . and I'm proud to be your commander. That's all."

"Troops . . . At-ten-tion!"

With a lightness in his tread that had not been present since the first Legionnaire died in the Costa Rican campaign, General Norman Stand Watie walked to the waiting staff car. *Yes*, he thought, *the Legion's future is assured.* And so is theirs, at least for a while.